Elizabeth Coke is not prepared to wait three years to obtain a divorce from her husband, a solicitor named (appropriately) Edward Coke. She claims to have been treated with 'exceptional depravity' and to prove this in the divorce courts she has enlisted the services of no less a person than Sir Nicholas Harding, Q.C.

Meanwhile Coke himself is ready for litigation against his wife, in the form of a libel case. She has written a letter to a friend in which she describes the 'exceptional depravity' of which she complains; the letter has been shown to friends and therefore – technically – published. The barrister of Coke's choice is Antony Maitland, Q.C., Sir Nicholas Harding's nephew.

The libel case is likely to be heard before the divorce case and thus the outcome will be decisive for both. Therefore Sir Nicholas has to defend the libel case against his nephew, and this remarkable confrontation does in fact occur – with sensational results.

Subsequently there is a double murder for Maitland to investigate.

This is one of the most dazzling of Sara Woods's many successful plots, a fine thriller and whodunnit that will enthrall many readers.

by the same author

ENTER A GENTLEWOMAN

Sara Woods

'Enter a Gentlewoman'
(Stage direction)

Coriolanus, Act I, Scene iii

Macmillan

ISBN: 0 333 32393 9

First published 1982 by
MACMILLAN LONDON LIMITED
London and Basingstoke
Associated companies in Auckland, Dallas, Delhi,
Dublin, Hong Kong, Johannesburg, Lagos, Manzini,
Melbourne, Nairobi, New York, Singapore, Tokyo,
Washington and Zaria

Typeset in Great Britain by
MB GRAPHIC SERVICES LIMITED
Bovingdon, Hertfordshire

Printed in Great Britain by
THE ANCHOR PRESS LIMITED
Tiptree, Essex

Bound in Great Britain by
WM. BRENDON AND SON LIMITED
Tiptree, Essex

Any work of fiction whose characters were of uniform excellence
would rightly be condemned – by that fact if by no other – as
being incredibly dull. Therefore no excuse can be considered
necessary for the villainy or folly of the people appearing in this
book. It seems extremely unlikely that any of them should
resemble a real person, alive or dead. Any such resemblance is
completely unintentional and without malice.

S. W.

PART I

EASTER TERM, 1973

Prologue

'I just don't believe it,' said Antony Maitland flatly. He was standing in his favourite position with his back to the fire place in the big, comfortable, rather shabby living room of the flat he and his wife occupied at the top of his uncle's house in Kempenfeldt Square, and his tone was completely incredulous. Which, as Sir Nicholas Harding pointed out with equal vehemence, was ridiculous in a man of his profession, who should be inured, after so many years at the bar, to any vagaries the human race might care to display.

'But ... divorce,' said Antony blankly. 'You've never touched a divorce case in your life and you've always said—'

'There are circumstances,' said his uncle, leaning back in his chair and obviously well satisfied with the result of his bombshell, 'that alter even the most strictly held rules.'

'But it isn't your kind of thing,' Maitland protested. 'What do you know about divorce anyway?'

'Enough to disapprove of it,' said Sir Nicholas blandly, with a glance at his wife of nearly two years' standing that in a less dignified man might almost have been called doting. Lady Harding, who, until her marriage, had been Miss Vera Langhorne, Barrister-at-law, returned the look with her rather grim smile, and then turned to her nephew to add her weight to her husband's arguments.

'Take it from me, Antony, not a usual case.'

'No, of course,' said Antony rather impatiently. 'None of them are.' But at this point, to the surprise of all of them, his wife interrupted him.

Jenny Maitland was also in her favourite place, curled up

7

in one corner of the sofa. Dinner was over, coffee had been drunk and cognac distributed – it was a Tuesday evening when the Maitlands traditionally entertained the Hardings – and for at least six weeks life had been running smoothly. She was always a better listener than a talker, and had been looking and feeling as relaxed as a kitten before the fire, but now she roused herself to expostulate. 'It isn't reasonable, Uncle Nick,' she said, 'and what's more it isn't fair. You've been lecturing us for years on marital fidelity and domestic harmony, even though we haven't given you the slightest reason. And now you're going to embroil yourself in someone else's troubles.'

'There are things,' said Sir Nicholas, 'that no human being should be asked to accept. The lady who is my client–'

'Oh, it's a woman, is it?' Antony and Jenny exchanged a look, because they knew well enough that for all his long bachelorhood there wasn't a woman living who couldn't twist Sir Nicholas round her little finger if she set her mind to it. Until he got her into court that is, when his attitude might be quite different.

Vera said gruffly into the silence that followed, 'Ought to give Nicholas a chance to explain.' She had at the best of times an elliptical way of speaking, intensified when anything moved her; and though she was used by now, after two years in the same household and many years previously of professional contact, to the frequent arguments between uncle and nephew, still she occasionally constituted herself as peacemaker.

'Well, of course I want to know,' said Antony. '*All* about it,' he added, in case there should be any mistake about that. 'To begin with, Uncle Nick, there's the question I asked you a moment ago, what do you know about divorce?'

'If you mean about the mechanics of the matter,' said Sir

8

Nicholas, 'very little. My instructing solicitor however –'

'Yes, who got you into this?'

'Our friend, Mr Bellerby.'

'But you know all his geese are swans,' said Maitland on a rising note of alarm. 'If he's persuaded you –'

'I know Bellerby quite as well as you do,' his uncle retorted. 'Rather better in fact, and for a longer period. However, I've sufficient sense of preservation to have insisted on seeing my client as well. And what she told me persuaded me that this was an instance where there must be a separation. I tried to persuade her, in fact, that this would be sufficient if legally arranged, but she said she'd never feel safe again unless the break was complete.'

'I still don't see why they need you,' Antony grumbled. 'In these days the whole thing can be got over in a few minutes, can't it?'

'A petition will not be considered until three years after the marriage,' his uncle told him. 'That doesn't apply in this case. In any case, the suit is being very strenuously contested.'

'Wait a bit!' A suspicion was dawning in Maitland's mind. 'What's the name of this damsel in distress of yours?'

'The description is hardly one that appeals to me,' said Sir Nicholas austerely. 'A young woman, certainly. In her late twenties I should say.'

'That's all very well, but what's her name?'

'Elizabeth Coke.'

'Oh lord!' Antony abandoned his place on the hearth rug and sank into the wing chair at the other side of the fireplace from the one his uncle occupied. 'That's torn it,' he said.

'My dear boy, if you must express yourself in this casual way –'

'Never mind that for the moment.' Antony interrupted his uncle ruthlessly. 'Mallory informed me today he's accepted a brief for me in a libel action.'

'Well?'

This time it was Jenny and Vera who exchanged glances, Jenny's purely bewildered, but Vera quite definitely amused. 'Going to tell us the name of your client, Antony?' she asked. She was a tall woman, addicted to sack-like clothing that made her look larger than ever, though since her marriage she had acquired a sense of colour that had been lacking before. Beside her, Jenny looked very slender; one might have thought they hadn't much in common but they had become firm allies.

'Of course I am,' Maitland was saying. 'He's a solicitor called Edward Coke, and he's suing his wife, Elizabeth.'

'One might almost suspect that Mallory is developing a sense of humour,' said Sir Nicholas reflectively. 'What is the alleged libel?'

'I don't know the details yet, but I gather it arises from the things she's saying to get the court to consider her petition before the three years are up. She's got to establish – what's the phrase? – exceptional depravity. Being, as I understand it, a family solicitor, that wouldn't do him much good.'

'Who's briefing you?' asked Sir Nicholas.

'A chap called Desmond Barleycorn, of all things. He's Coke's junior partner, and is representing him.'

'I suppose both he and you know,' said Sir Nicholas, 'that any communications that Mrs Coke makes to her lawyers or to the court are privileged.'

'Of course I know it,' said Antony, impatient again. 'You've rebuked me often enough, Uncle Nick, for theorising ahead of my data, and now you're doing it yourself.'

'What do you mean?'

'Merely that the action is based on a letter Elizabeth wrote to a friend of hers. But I told you I don't know any details yet.'

'But as for the divorce action, I gather we shan't be facing each other in court over that.'

'No, but —'

'Nothing has been said to me yet about libel,' said Sir Nicholas. He was a tall man, rather more heavily built than his nephew, with hair so fair that the fact that it was gradually whitening could hardly be distinguished, and an air of authority of which he was completely unconscious.

'No, but I bet it will,' Antony told him. 'It's only just arisen I believe.'

'Amusing situation,' said Vera. 'Think I shall attend the court.'

'I shall be sorry to disappoint you, my dear,' said Sir Nicholas, 'but I'm not at all sure that Antony should accept this case.' He looked straight at his nephew. 'Being a civil matter it's quite open to you to refuse the brief.'

'Why should I do that?'

'Because quite frankly I think your proposed client deserves all that's coming to him, and I should prefer you not to become involved with a man of his type.'

'I'm not likely to be harmed by the association,' said Maitland amused in his turn. 'In any case, I should prefer to make my own judgment of the matter.'

'You haven't seen him then?'

'No, he's coming to chambers tomorrow with Barleycorn. About eleven o'clock as far as I remember.'

'Well, I hope you'll bear what I've said in mind. If Mrs Coke is to be believed — and I do believe her implicitly — he's a thoroughly bad lot.'

'Yes, Uncle Nick, but she may not be telling the truth.'

'It wasn't a story she liked telling, not an edifying story,' his uncle elaborated. 'I think the fact that she forced herself to tell it at all, first to Bellerby and then to me, shows that she was completely desperate.'

'There might be more reasons than one for that.'

11

'Who's theorising ahead of his data now?' said Vera suddenly. 'Think you ought to listen to your uncle, Antony.'

'Of course I will, I always do,' he added, with the sudden smile that emphasised the humorous look that was characteristic of him, 'because I've no choice in the matter, but when it comes down to it I've got to make my own decision.'

'Stubborn,' she commented.

'Yes, perhaps. Will you tell me what she said that made you think her deserving of your help, Uncle Nick? Or under the circumstances do you think it improper for us to discuss it?'

'There's no reason that I can see why I shouldn't give you an outline of the story,' said Sir Nicholas. 'If we are to meet in court, however, I imagine we shall each of us wish to keep the details of our strategy to ourselves.'

'Yes, of course. As Vera says, it ought to be amusing.' Antony was beginning to feel uneasy, and trying hard not to show it. 'What is this exceptional depravity that demonstrates the irretrievable breakdown of their marriage?'

For the first time Sir Nicholas hesitated. 'It's not a pretty story,' he said.

'So you've already told us,' said Antony, unmoved.

'Well –' He glanced doubtfully at Jenny. 'I think perhaps it would be more suitable if we discussed the matter in chambers, Antony.'

'Really, Uncle Nick,' said Jenny rather huffily. 'I'm not a child, you know.'

'No, my dear. But you are not perhaps quite so familiar with the ways of the world as the rest of us are. Even Vera, because of her profession.'

'I haven't been living in this house all these years and remained a complete innocent,' said Jenny. Then she grinned at him. 'Things that might have been put differently,' she said, 'but you know what I mean.'

'I think I know,' said Sir Nicholas returning her smile. Jenny was one of the people it was hard not to smile at. 'Have you ever heard of Adelaide Bartlett?'

'Of course I have, Uncle Nick, I've read all about her.'

'Then perhaps the story won't come as too much of a shock to you.'

'But it isn't a murder we're talking about,' Jenny protested.

'No, my dear, I'm referring to the Bartletts' life before the husband was killed. You may remember that there was a young clergyman involved with Adelaide. It has never been quite clear to me from my reading how far matters went, but what is certain is that Bartlett thoroughly approved of the matter, spoke of the young man as his wife's future husband, and encouraged them in every way.'

'Yes I know all about that,' said Jenny. 'Is that what you're making such a fuss about? That this Mr Coke has been encouraging his wife to have an affair with somebody else?'

'Not exactly,' said Sir Nicholas. For all her protestations, Jenny had retained an air of innocence, and Sir Nicholas himself would have admitted to some inhibitions where what was once known as the weaker sex were concerned. 'If I resort to a modern colloquialism you must forgive me, because I find myself quite at a loss how to word it otherwise. There's a young man, a friend of the family, who is in love with Mrs Coke though she doesn't return his affections. It pleased the husband to force his wife into a relationship with this man against her will.'

'That's all very well, but where does the modern colloquialism come in?' Antony demanded.

'If you will have it, Coke – got his kicks, do they say? – out of seeing the couple indulge in sexual intercourse in his presence, even though he himself had never seen fit to consummate his marriage. What do you say to that?'

'I should say the young man you spoke of – the third party – must be a pretty queer fish,' said Antony bluntly.

'Very probably, but that's not the point. Nor does my one lapse excuse your constant use of slang. However,' he added magnanimously, 'let that pass for the moment. The point is that my client found the position intolerable, and is seeking the only remedy available to her. I may say she struck me as a completely truthful and straightforward person, and in great distress.'

'Yes, I can imagine that.'

'If you're going to be sarcastic–'

'That wasn't sarcasm, Uncle Nick, it was the simple truth. All the same –'

'Can't deny him the opportunity of talking to the man,' said Vera, seeing her husband about to interrupt. 'For his own opinion, only way.'

'I suppose so,' said Sir Nicholas grudgingly, but this time he smiled. 'Have you noticed anything about the name of your client, Antony?'

'A very suitable name for a lawyer,' said Antony grinning. 'And now the poor chap is going to be exposed himself to the gladsome light of jurisprudence. I don't suppose the name of his illustrious predecessor comforts him at all.'

'No, I don't suppose so either,' said Sir Nicholas and picked up his brandy glass. 'Well, you'll see this fellow tomorrow, Antony, and I wish you joy of the meeting. Though I must admit to a few regrets myself when I heard what happened.'

'Why, if the lady is so attractive?'

'That,' said his uncle with dignity, 'has nothing to do with the case. It's an old firm, Coke, Coke and Barleycorn.'

'Never heard of them.'

'Most likely you wouldn't, it's purely a family practice. This Coke is the second one I believe, I knew his father quite well but he died some years ago. I'm sorry now it never occurred to me to ask him whether he chose his son's Christian name deliberately.'

'Is Edward like Adelaide Barlett's husband, an older man?'

'I believe she said he's ten years her senior, which should put him in his late thirties. Not too big a difference.'

'I see.' He got up again, restless now, and went across to the table where the decanters were set out. 'Who lives may learn' he said casually. 'We may both be wiser by this time tomorrow night.'

Wednesday, 9th May

I

Desmond Barleycorn and Edward Coke arrived at Sir Nicholas Harding's chambers in the Inner Temple about ten minutes before the appointed time. Antony, who was struggling with a set of papers concerning the obtaining of pecuniary advantage by deception – and thoroughly agreeing with the designation of the statute as a judicial nightmare, even though it had been amended since that description was applied to it – was glad enough to push his work to one side and tell Willett to show them in immediately. His room was long and narrow and rather dark even on the sunniest day. That morning was far from sunny, and he went to the door to augment the light from his table lamp with that of the ceiling fixture before his visitors arrived.

In spite of what his uncle had told him he had been expecting an older man. Edward Coke, coming into the room before his partner and representative, was a tall man who looked no more than in his middle thirties. Dark and with regular features that might almost have been considered handsome. A very conservative looking man both in his dress and grooming, it was easy to see that the allegation of perversion might hurt him badly both professionally and personally. His appearance, Maitland thought, was one point in his favour, it remained to be seen what else he had to say for himself.

Desmond Barleycorn was obviously several years his junior, and equally obviously modelled himself on his partner though without too much success. He had an eager manner, his hair was sandy and had a distinct tendency to wave, and altogether he looked as if he would have been more comfortable in country clothes than in the conventional garb his city practice required of him. He came past Coke now with his hand outstretched. 'Mr Maitland,' he said, 'I'm very glad to make your acquaintance. This is my partner, Edward Coke.'

Antony accepted his hand will-nilly – Coke didn't offer his – acknowledged the introduction and waved his two visitors to chairs. The ceiling light gave him a pretty good view of them both, without creating the impression that he was about to embark on the third degree. 'The floor is yours, Mr Barleycorn,' he said, placing the onus of the interview neatly where he felt it belonged.

The solicitor, who had been only too obviously taking stock of him – a tall man with a casual manner, dark hair, grey eyes, and a thin, intelligent face – came to with a start. 'Yes, yes, of course. Do you think you could manage to call me Desmond? It's such a stupid name,' said Barleycorn. 'I sometimes think of changing it, but that's so complicated, nobody knows who you are any more.'

'Yes, I can imagine the difficulties. Now I haven't had a chance to go through the papers thoroughly yet,' – in point of fact he hadn't been near them – 'but in any case I have a weakness for hearing things at first hand. However, I understand we can't consider the matter altogether without also considering the suit your wife is bringing against you for divorce.'

'That's right.' Edward Coke spoke for the first time, except for the mutter of greeting he had given on arrival. His voice was unexpectedly deep and attractive. Given a little more animation you could have imagined him an actor rather than as a member of the legal profession.

'But my clerk tells me you only require my services in the matter of the libel.'

'There've been some developments,' said Desmond.

'Something I should know about?'

'It doesn't make any difference to the facts, but we had thought that the divorce action would come on first. However, it seems that, being a contested case, there will be a good deal of delay, and the libel action is liable to be heard first. When the verdict is in, in effect the divorce petition will be decided too.'

'I see. I think I ought to tell you that my uncle, Sir Nicholas Harding, has been briefed by Mrs Coke's solicitor. That was merely to take care of the divorce, but it seems likely that his help will also be requested in the other matter.'

'That may be a bit awkward for you,' said Barleycorn, 'but I don't see what difference it makes to us. There's no objection to members of the same chambers, or even of the same family, appearing on opposite sides in court.'

'No, that's true, but I felt I should mention it. But it brings us to another matter' – a smile took the sting out of the words – 'that I think our client can only answer for himself. If the divorce weren't contested, Mr Coke, there would be no need for these allegations that distress you so much to be made public. Mrs Coke could wait until the three years are up, and then petition in the usual way on the grounds of the irretrievable breakdown of the marriage.'

'I don't believe in divorce,' said Edward Coke simply.

'Is that on religious grounds?'

'I'm a Catholic. Elizabeth came into the church before we were married, so there's no question of the legality of our marriage from the religious, not the secular, point of view, which is what concerns me.'

'Have you considered – if I'm talking out of turn you must forgive me, Mr Coke, but it's my duty to advise you that you might obtain a dispensation to grant your wife a divorce, since the consequences of opposing her may be so serious to yourself?'

'I have not considered it.'

'I can quite see that you wouldn't feel yourself free to remarry, but –'

'It would be distortion of everything I believe. I'll never consent to giving Elizabeth her own way in this without a fight.'

'And you think that if you can make good your claim to have been libelled –'

'The divorce action would fall to the ground. There can be no question about that.'

'That brings us to the point then, do you think you can make it stick?' He was looking at Desmond Barleycorn now, and it was the younger man who answered him.

'As far as proving specific damages is concerned it's quite straightforward. And as far as proving that the damaging statements were committed to paper and published in the legal sense that's quite straightforward too. But –' He hesitated.

'The defence of truth is open to Mrs Coke,' said Maitland. 'Is that what you mean?'

'That's exactly what I mean.' Barleycorn sounded relieved. 'That's why –' He hesitated again. Some of his earlier eagerness seemed to have left him. 'That's why I told Edward we must have you,' he said then, obviously taking his courage into both hands.

'Why?' asked Maitland uncompromisingly.

'Because I know your reputation, of course.'

This was a statement that Antony had heard many times in the past, and that always annoyed him. Besides a professional bias against publicity, he had a very personal hatred of it as well, and he disliked the reminder of the attention that the newspapers sometimes had given to his activities. 'In connection with criminal matters,' he said now sharply. 'You can't possibly have heard of my ever concerning myself with domestic affairs of this kind.'

'Forget the domestic angle then, if it makes you any happier,' said Desmond obligingly. 'You've been engaged in libel actions before, don't tell me you haven't. This is just like any other, if you forget that the protagonists are man and wife.'

'Unfortunately that seems to be the whole gist of the matter,' said Maitland rather discontentedly. 'However, do I gather that you're telling me that if Mrs Coke claims the truth of her statement we can't prove anything to the contrary.'

'As things stand at the moment,' said Desmond. 'But you see, Mr Maitland, people say you can see further through a brick wall than most of us, so I was hoping –'

'That I should see my way to carrying my enquiries a little further than the mere acceptance of the brief commits me to,' said Maitland. He paused, considering the matter. 'Well . . . that's fair enough I suppose from your point of view, but there's my point of view to be considered too.'

'You're thinking of the time it will take.'

'Not altogether.'

'He's thinking,' said Edward Coke in his deep voice, 'that when he's heard my story he may not believe it.'

'Oh, I say!' Desmond seemed thrown off his stroke for a moment by this plain speaking, but then he saw that Maitland's expression had lightened.

'That's exactly what I was thinking, Mr Coke,' said Antony cordially. 'So perhaps you'd better get to the purpose of this meeting. Are you going to tell me . . . or would you rather Mr Barleycorn spoke for you?'

'Desmond knows as much about the matter as I do, of course,' said Edward Coke, 'but then I know as much about the legal position as he does so I may as well tell you myself. Have you gathered from the material Desmond

20

sent you the nature of the charge Elizabeth is making against me?'

'I know about it in outline, yes,' said Antony, adhering to the truth as well as he could without mentioning his talk with his uncle.

'Then perhaps we needn't go into that any further for the moment.'

'No, but there's the question of publication of the libel.'

'Of course you must be wondering about that. Elizabeth went to her solicitor, who may be known to you –'

'Mr Bellerby? Yes, very well known indeed.'

'Well, I can only guess the course of that first interview. I imagine he told her the difficulties of obtaining a divorce when we'd only been married for two and a half years. And I don't know how she put it, but she told him she could establish good reason for making the petition at this time, and then she went back to see him and took David Barrie with her. He is the chap I'm supposed to ... she's supposed to ... well anyway, he agreed with everything she said. And she must have got this Mr Bellerby completely hoodwinked, because apparently he told her she had a watertight case, and I admit if it were true it would be watertight. And Elizabeth was foolish enough to write to a bosom friend of hers, Primrose Ross – who is herself a very silly woman, though not a bad sort apart from that – a sort of gloating letter. "We've got him just where we want him," things like that, and going on to tell the whole unsavoury story.'

'And this Mrs – Miss? – Ross came to you with the letter?'

'It's Miss Ross. No, that isn't exactly how it was. She just talked about it to at least two couples we all know, Roland and Frances Walpole, and Terence and Joanna Stowe. It was Roland who told me about it, he and Fran didn't believe a word of it. At least that's what he said and I think

21

he was telling the truth. But Terence and Joanna were obviously avoiding me, so I made a point of getting hold of him and tackling him about it. After a while he admitted that Primrose had spoken to them, and they'd mentioned the story to several other people. I don't know how many that means, but perhaps if you ask them they'd tell you. Both those couples could testify, though I have a feeling Terence and Joanna would do so unwillingly, and the tale is certainly one that would harm me professionally, apart from my feelings in the matter. My conversation with Terence was followed by a stiff little note, which must have been already in the post when we talked, asking us to hand over his affairs to another firm. But I was explaining, I also talked to Primrose.'

'And she admitted receiving the letter?'

'She did more than that, she gave it to me. I told you she was a very silly woman, I don't think she had the faintest idea she was harming Elizabeth by doing so.' He paused and smiled a little. 'I'm beginning to believe you when you say you haven't studied your brief, Mr Maitland. There's a copy of the letter there.'

'Yes, but you see –'

'You're not sure even now that you're going to take the case. I understand that perfectly. And you're going to remind me that unless we can prove Elizabeth is lying what Primrose did won't harm her in any way, except to get her into court, which is a thing nobody likes I suppose. But if she gets a verdict in the libel business, the divorce is as good as in her pocket.'

'Yes, and that's the next point I'm puzzled about. If her story isn't true, Mr Coke, why does she want a divorce? You said you'd only been married ... what is it, two and a half years?'

'Something like that. December 1970 to be exact. And as for why she wants a divorce ... I think she finds marriage

22

distasteful, we haven't slept together since the very early days. But I can't see her reason for going to these lengths.'

'Did she talk the matter over with you before going to see Mr Bellerby?'

'Yes, she asked me for a divorce right out. I told her, of course, what she knew perfectly well already, that as Catholics that course wasn't open to us, and she just told me not to be so stuffy. I offered her a separation, and to go on supporting her as though we were still living together, but that wouldn't do for her at all. We argued about it for quite a time, or rather she did, and then she went away breathing threats, and packed her bag and went to an hotel. The next thing I knew the divorce papers were served on me. Of course, in view of the length of time we'd been married I knew she must be claiming exceptional hardship of some kind, but I didn't quite realise what entered into it until Roland came to see me. I admit that shook me up.'

'And there's no word of truth in her allegations?'

'No truth at all. Think a minute, Mr Maitland –'

'I am thinking,' said Antony rather ruefully.

'– if I were the sort of man, I suppose I should say the sort of pervert she describes, do you think I'd allow my religion to get in the way of giving her a divorce without scandal?'

'It's a good point.'

'Not altogether convincing,' said Coke. 'If people were always logical . . . we're not, and I know that as well as you do. I can only assure you –'

'He's telling the truth, you know,' said Desmond Barleycorn, coming back unexpectedly into the conversation.

'Tell me about David Barrie,' said Maitland abruptly.

'David?' Coke sounded startled.

'I should think it's obvious that I need to know something about him. You tell me you can give no explanation as to why Mrs Coke should be so insistent on a divorce. Perhaps you can explain to me though why this young man should back her up in a lying story?'

'I can't tell you that either,' said Edward Coke rather despairingly.

'Come on, have a stab at it,' said Maitland, falling into the vernacular in a way that his uncle would have instantly condemned. 'Is he a friend of the family? Has he been in the habit of visiting you?'

'I suppose you can say both he and his father are friends of ours, though as far as I'm concerned he's a younger man, just as Owen, his father, is much older than I am. Mrs Barrie died some years ago.'

'Friends of yours, or friends of Mrs Coke's?'

'Of both of us, I suppose. It used to be a matter of inviting them to dinner every so often, and of being invited back with equal regularity, but in the last six months or so, perhaps a little longer, David has taken to dropping in and taking what he calls pot luck with us. I didn't mind, Elizabeth seemed to enjoy his company, and to tell you the truth our relations were becoming so strained that the presence of a third party was something of a relief.'

'The first time he came –?'

'That was at Elizabeth's invitation. At least, I think she'd told him he'd be welcome at any time. She said Owen was worried about his – about David's – way of life, and she thought these visits with us might give his mind another direction. Of course, when she put it like that I couldn't refuse to have him about the place, much as I should have liked to.'

'Still you can't deny the three of you were alone together.'

'No, and we haven't a live-in servant so you've no chance of getting evidence there.'

'How old is David Barrie? What is his occupation?'

'I'd say about thirty, not too much older than Elizabeth.

24

And Owen is a very wealthy man, I don't think David has ever done a stroke of work in his life. I suppose he's what you'd call a dilettante. Attends all the first nights, all the art shows –'

'And is said to have agreed to these rather odd proceedings because he is in love with your wife.'

'I dare say he is. Obviously I'd be the last person to know.'

'An odd kind of love. And Mrs Coke's feelings in the matter?'

'She says she was frightened of me,' said Edward bitterly, 'and that's why she agreed.'

'Have you ever struck her, for instance?'

'I have not.'

'I didn't mean that, in any case. I meant, what could you tell me about her feelings for David Barrie?'

'That's something I should have been the last person to know too, if she's in love with him I mean. But honestly, Mr Maitland, I think it very unlikely. On the surface she appears a warm loving woman, but underneath I have to say she's frigid.'

'I see. But I have to point out to you Mr Coke, that if you're telling me the truth she has taken in not only Mr Bellerby, who is very far from being a fool, but also my uncle who is one of the astutest men I know.'

'Then you don't believe me.' Edward Coke began to get to his feet, but Maitland waved him back to his chair impatiently.

'Don't go so fast,' he implored. 'I didn't say anything of the kind you know.' And he smiled to himself as he spoke, remembering that Geoffrey Horton had told him that he never got rough with his clients unless he was beginning to believe them. In this case he was finding that his own feelings were at war with his respect for his uncle's judgement, but there was his prospective client's point of view as well.

If he was the upright man he seemed, and his wife's story a cruel invention, he would suffer terribly if it obtained general credence, and not only in his professional life. 'Tell me from the beginning about your relationship with Mrs Coke,' Antony invited.

Edward had sunk back into his chair again but he had a doubtful look. 'She was twenty-five when we were married, twenty-eight now, her birthday was last week as a matter of fact,' he said. 'And I was thirty-five, too old for her you may think. But before I met her I hadn't seen anybody I could consider sharing my whole life with. As you may have gathered, Mr Maitland, for me it was a life-time commitment.'

'Yes, I had gathered that,' said Antony seriously.

'She was nurse-companion to an old aunt of mine when I met her,' Edward went on. 'I was fond of Aunt Harriet but I know she could be trying, and Elizabeth was so gentle with her, I think that was the first thing that attracted me to her. She's . . . I think you could call her a beauty, Mr Maitland, I can't think really how she'd gone so long unattached. Anyway, we were married after about four months.'

'What did your aunt think about that?'

'Oh, she seemed as pleased as could be. That's why I was so surprised . . . but that's beside the point.'

'What were you going to say, Mr Coke?'

'Only that she died last year, late November I think it was, and left all her money to charity. I suppose she thought I didn't need it, which is perfectly true in a way, though I'm not a wealthy man. She was,' he added rather ruefully. 'Wealthy, I mean.'

'Go on about your marriage.'

'I've already told you all there is to tell. For the first few weeks . . . but I believe now that Elizabeth was only humouring me. Then she began to make excuses, and finally she moved into another room altogether, and quite simply wouldn't let me near her. Our day-to-day life went on as it had done before, but you can imagine, I suppose, that what I had imagined to be our affection for each other began to fade, and our relationship grew more and more strained. I wasn't surprised when she wanted a separation, but the thought of divorce had never entered my head.'

'That reminds me of something you left out, Mr Coke. You say Mrs Coke was not a Catholic when you met her.'

'No, but I think – I thought then – that she was of a religious frame of mind. Anyway, she agreed quite readily to go for instruction, that delayed our marriage a little bit but not much.'

'From what you've told me it hardly delayed it at all,' said Antony smiling.

'No, I suppose our original courtship was rather brief,' Edward agreed.

'And after your marriage?'

'At first we went to church together, then she decided she'd rather go to a later mass. I've wondered since whether perhaps she didn't go at all, but visited a friend instead.'

'This Primrose Ross for instance.'

'Well, yes, she'd be as likely as any other. But if you're thinking, Mr Maitland, that her attitude to sex was coloured by . . . by, say, any lesbian tendencies, I think I can assure you that there was nothing of the kind.'

'You say David Barrie has money?'

'I suppose you could say he has, but not really of his own. A good allowance from his father, I imagine, who disapproves of anybody who doesn't work, but has a soft spot for his son all the same.'

'Are there any other brothers and sisters? Or could David expect to be his sole heir?'

'He has no other family, but damn it all, Owen is only in his middle fifties.'

'I see.' He turned to smile at Desmond Barleycorn. 'And if I look at those papers you sent me I shall find the names and addresses of all these people,' he said.

'That means you're going to see them?' Desmond asked eagerly.

'I think that seems to be called for, don't you?'

'Yes, but I don't know what good it will do,' said Desmond honestly.

'It's a beginning, that's all, unless you can suggest anywhere else I should look.'

'No . . . no. You can't talk to David Barrie, I suppose.'

'I can talk to his father though. And if I were you, Mr Barleycorn – Desmond – I'd send Miss Primrose Ross a *subpoena* immediately.'

'I thought of that but I don't see that it matters much which side calls her. She's our witness as far as the receipt of the letter is concerned, but she's so pally with Elizabeth I wouldn't mind betting she'll back up any story of hers. And her evidence on top of David's is just what we don't need.'

'No, but the advantage of my going to see her before the trial might outweigh all that. As you say, in any case she'll have a chance of getting over Mrs Coke's point of view.'

'All right, I'll do that. Do you want me to arrange appointments?'

Maitland considered. 'Yes, I suppose we should go on this expedition hand in hand,' he said at last lightly, though all his instincts were for conducting his interviews alone. 'If you wouldn't mind consulting with Willett, in the clerk's office, on your way out . . . Mallory is our clerk you know, but Willett is more or less second in command and takes a good deal off his shoulders these days. Anyway, he knows my case load, and he knows my appointments. Would you do that?'

'With the greatest of pleasure.' Both men had come to their feet now and Antony got up too.

'I'm a little bewildered,' said Edward, frowning. 'In the absence of any evidence at all I'd expected you to turn me down without further ado.'

'My family would tell you I'm of a contrary disposition,' said Antony lightly, and smiled again to himself, thinking of Jenny who wouldn't have said anything of the kind. 'You do realise though, that I'm not promising I can help you. Only that I'll try.'

'For the moment I think that's good enough,' said Edward with more warmth in his tone than had been there before. 'You've made things very easy for me, Mr Maitland, easier than I would have believed possible, so let me be grateful for that at least.'

Maitland remained on his feet for a moment after the door closed behind them, staring at it rather blankly. He was wondering rather ruefully what had induced him to agree to investigating this rather sordid matter, but it cannot be denied that at the back of his mind there was also a query as to how his uncle would take this aligning himself with the opposite camp. Either Edward Coke or Elizabeth his wife was the liar of the century, and at that moment he wouldn't have taken even the smallest bet on the answer to that conundrum either way.

II

'But, Antony, are you sure?' said Jenny that evening when he had finished telling her about his talk with Desmond Barleycorn and his client. 'I mean, you know, Uncle Nick is really an awfully good judge of character himself.'

'I know he is, and of course I'm not sure,' said Antony. 'Only you know, love, if Edward Coke does happen to be telling the truth . . . well I can hardly take a chance on that, can I?'

'Being you,' said Jenny, 'I suppose you can't. But there are two things that worry me about it.'

'One, I suppose,' said Antony resignedly, 'is what Uncle Nick is going to say. Well, I talked to him at lunch today, and he was pretty scathing about my credulous nature, but the rest doesn't matter really. He knows perfectly well I've a right to accept whatever clients I choose.'

'Yes, I dare say,' said Jenny doubtfully. 'And if he's right I don't think it will matter at all. You'll have wasted your time and that will be all there is to it. But supposing *you're* right?'

'I don't think you're doing him justice, Jenny. You know as well as I do a barrister's life is full of ups and downs, none of us can be right all the time. So what's the other thing that's worrying you?'

'If this Mr Coke is telling you the truth,' said Jenny, 'how on earth are you going to prove it? The kind of things his wife says were going on aren't exactly public performances, and if she and David Barrie stick to their stories there's nothing you can do about it.'

'I don't suppose there is, but at least I can have the satisfaction of trying.'

'If that was all there was to it,' said Jenny.

'What on earth do you mean, love?'

'Just that I know you, Antony, only too well. You'll blame yourself for failing, and never have a moment's peace again,' said Jenny tragically.

'Come now, love, it's not as bad as all that.' But Jenny was pursuing her own train of thought.

'If Uncle Nick's wrong,' she said, 'how do you think he could have been so taken in?'

'From all accounts Elizabeth Coke is pretty hot stuff,' said Antony. 'Edward Coke – accepting his story for the moment – was taken in himself, and he had a good deal more at stake than Uncle Nick has. He was committing himself to a lifetime with the woman.'

'And if she gets her divorce eventually he still won't remarry?'

'I don't know if he wants to, but in any case I don't think he will. I suppose that's really what inclined me to his side, Jenny. If he's telling the truth about that, and I think he is, the divorce won't be the slightest use to him. He doesn't know what's in it for Elizabeth either, but I can't help feeling there's something.'

'To get out of an intolerable situation, Uncle Nick thinks,' said Jenny. But Antony's thoughts too had gone off in another direction.

'I know the whole business is unsavoury,' he admitted, 'but it's fascinating all the same.'

'Is it?' said Jenny doubtfully.

'Of course it is, love. Think of David Barrie for instance. Whoever is telling the truth, what sort of a man is he?'

'Horrid, I should think,' said Jenny. 'And you say the libel case is coming on before the divorce?'

'Yes, I was a bit surprised about that but it seems to be so. That's something else I didn't tell you Jenny, Uncle Nick said at lunch time that Bellerby has asked him to take care of that too.'

'Vera will be pleased,' said Jenny.

'Will she? Why?'

'I think it will tickle that rather grim sense of humour of hers,' said Jenny, 'to see the two of you in opposition. Perhaps I'll come with her,' she added.

'No, I shouldn't do that, love, you wouldn't like it at all.'

Jenny smiled at him. 'All right, I won't,' she promised. 'But let's talk about something else now. I'm tired of what Uncle Nick calls marital discord, and I'm very tired,' she added firmly, 'of that phrase you and he were throwing at each other all last evening, exceptional depravity.'

I

As it happened it was the following Saturday before Maitland, through his faithful shadow Willett, was able to accept any of the suggestions Desmond Barleycorn put forward for the desired interviews. 'I have everything lined up,' the young solicitor said at last, 'but I'd like to talk to you first, if I may.'

'Yes of course,' said Antony vaguely, though he was wondering a little what could remain to be said between them. 'What time is our first appointment?'

'At eleven o'clock, with Owen Barrie. He lives not very far from you.'

'Does he though? There aren't many of these houses left in private hands. I suggest then that you come here, about ten o'clock, then we can take as long or as short a time as we like over our talk.'

As when he had attended the conference in chambers, Desmond was a little earlier than the appointed hour. Jenny provided coffee and disappeared discreetly, leaving the two men facing each other across the empty hearth. 'If you prefer something stronger,' Antony suggested, when the other man seemed to hesitate over how to open the conversation.

'Not at this time, thank you.' Desmond grinned at him. 'Though I admit it might oil the wheels a little if that's what you're thinking. You see, being Edward's partner I know rather more about him than the usual solicitor-client relationship. But I don't like talking behind his back.'

'That's very understandable.'

'All the same, there are things I think you should know. I mean, we're trusting you, aren't we, to pull us out of this mess?'

'You can trust me to try,' said Antony firmly. 'As for the rest –'

'Yes, I know you can't guarantee results,' said Desmond a little impatiently. 'And to tell you the truth I think Elizabeth has got us cold. Still, we have to do our best, and I do want you to understand a few things about Edward, that you may believe from me while you'd take them with a grain of salt from him.'

'I'm all attention,' said Antony idly, stirring his coffee.

'Yes, I've noticed that you seem to have the knack of hearing things, even when you don't seem to be listening. Well then, that business of not believing in divorce . . . he's perfectly sincere about that. He's that rarity nowadays, a genuinely religious man, and finds the doings of the so-called permissive society pretty objectionable. I'd already pointed out to him what you told him yourself, that it might be possible to get a dispensation, and there'd be no obligation on him to regard himself as anything but still married. But it's no use, he's completely obstinate about that, it's against his beliefs and that's that.'

'I'm glad to have your confirmation, of course,' Maitland told him. 'I gather you know the Cokes socially as well as being his partner.'

'Yes, of course. Old Mr Coke was alive when I entered the firm, in fact he gave me my articles, but Edward has always been very good and very helpful to me and I think as a matter of fact he'd have done better to get someone more experienced to represent him now, only he wouldn't hear of it,' concluded Desmond a little breathlessly.

'I'm sure you'll do very well.'

'I think I may, but only if you guide me every step of the way,' said Desmond frankly. 'You want to know what I

33

think of Elizabeth, don't you?'

'Well, all I can tell you, of course, is my own observation. Edward never mentioned her, except in the beginning that he was getting married, and later perhaps occasionally, "We enjoyed your company last night," something like that. I never actually met her until the wedding, she stayed on with the old lady right to the last minute and was married from her house, so as to be able to get the new nurse into her ways. It was a white wedding with all the trimmings and she looked absolutely stunning. I wasn't a bit surprised that Edward had fallen for her so hard, she has a gentle way with her that would also appeal to him. And I hadn't an idea, though this may be hard to credit, that anything was really wrong between them until all this blew up.'

'You say, "that anything was *really* wrong?" I take it then that you sensed something was amiss, but not that it was serious.'

'It's difficult to explain. You see, I think Edward is the sort of man who ought to have married someone his intellectual equal.'

'And Elizabeth isn't quite up to his weight?'

'Perhaps I put it the wrong way. She's certainly clever enough if she thought up this story all by herself, and I take it her solicitor had nothing to do with it.'

Antony had to smile. 'Mr Bellerby is the soul of respectability,' he assured his companion. 'If there's any deception going on I can assure you he's as much deceived as anyone.'

'That's what I thought. Anyway, it's not so much a matter of intellect or cleverness or whatever you like to call it as having the same interests,' Desmond explained. 'Edward is the sort of person who's interested in everything –'

'That ought to help.'

'No, I meant things like history and politics and

34

economics . . . everything except the sort of things Elizabeth likes. She's interested in fashion, and appearing in the right places at the right time in the right clothes. Do you understand what I mean?'

'Yes, I think I do. An unsuitable match, but even more disparate natures have made a go of it sometimes.'

'Yes, and that's what I thought they were doing. She'd become a Catholic, you know, and I'd no reason to believe she wasn't as sincere about that as Edward was. It was a bit of a shock when I heard she'd left him, that was before Edward told me himself. He didn't say a word about it until the divorce papers were served. And then all this!'

'Had you ever any idea that she found the physical side of marriage distasteful?'

'Not until recently.'

'Why do you think she wants a divorce?'

'It beats me,' said Desmond, shaking his head. 'If she just wants to get away from him a separation would have done just as well.'

'She may want to marry again.'

'You mean David Barrie?'

'If he's willing to perjure himself for her sake she must have some sort of a hold over him.'

'I've been thinking about that,' Desmond admitted. 'It may be that that small part of his story is true. That he's in love with her, I mean, but she doesn't care for him.'

'That just makes it odder than ever,' said Maitland thoughtfully. 'The only explanation I can think of is that she promised to marry him if she were free.'

'That would make more sense, I suppose.'

'Do you think she'd be capable of such a thing?'

'I have to believe it, haven't I, considering the story she's spreading? But I can't see why she'd want to change Edward for David.'

'She may not have meant it. After all, once the divorce is

35

granted she'll be quite free to go back on her promise.'

'And lay herself open to some pretty nasty insinuations from David.'

'She might not care. She might think nobody would believe him. Oh, I don't know,' said Maitland rather crossly. 'The whole thing's a mystery to me.'

'That's the worst thing they have against us, isn't it? The unlikelihood of anybody, particularly a gently-bred woman, telling such a story in public if it wasn't true.'

'Yes, I think you're right about that. Can you tell me anything about the other people involved, I wonder? David Barrie himself for instance?'

'I don't like him,' said Desmond uncompromisingly, 'and though I don't believe his story about Edward I have to admit that I think David would be capable of doing what he's said to have done.'

'What sort of an impression do you think he'll make in court?'

'They'll think he's a nasty piece of work and believe every word he says,' said Barleycorn.

'That's a pity. I suppose you know all the other people involved.'

'Yes, I've met them all at the Cokes' from time to time, but I don't know anything about them really, except that Primrose Ross is just as silly as Edward said. The other two couples both seem pleasant enough in their own way. But –'

'Yes?' said Antony encouragingly after a moment. 'You didn't come here just to tell me you believe our client's story, did you?'

'No, I came because I thought there's someone else you ought perhaps to see. A girl called Mary Jerrold.'

'That's a new name,' said Maitland casually, but his eyes had suddenly become intent.

'Yes,' agreed Desmond simply.

36

Antony waited a moment. 'And why should I want to talk to her?' he asked.

'Because she's very much in love with Edward and I'm afraid if Elizabeth gets into any difficulties over this she may drop Mary's name into it as well.'

'I see,' said Maitland slowly. And then, 'Tell me more,' he invited.

'Mary works in the office, she's a fully qualified solicitor but not a partner.'

'What is your concern with her, Desmond?'

'Just that she's a thoroughly nice person and I don't want her to be hurt. I don't want Edward to be hurt through her either.'

'Could he be?'

'Not in the sense you mean, I think. It's a perfectly innocent relationship. But after what Elizabeth is saying, I've no idea what she might come out with next.'

'I see. Has Mr Coke confided in you about this?'

'I don't even know if there's anything to confide. Mary talked to me, we work together a good deal and we're good friends, and though I suspect Edward may return her feelings I've no real knowledge of the fact. He's never said a word about it.'

'If Miss Jerrold is so open about her affection for him –'

'I don't think she's told anybody but me,' said Desmond hastily. 'Only I have to admit that the way she feels isn't exactly a secret. She's rather a transparent person.'

'And you think Mrs Coke may know?'

'It's the kind of thing she'd be on to like a flash,' said Desmond positively.

'That's a pity. Even so it may do more harm than good to talk to Miss Jerrold at this stage. Why exactly do you want me to see her?'

'To warn her to be careful. She won't listen to me,' said Desmond ruefully.

37

'I see. There is however, the fact that she might be glad enough if the divorce went through.'

'She knows perfectly well how Edward would feel about remarrying. You were talking about self-sacrifice a moment ago. That's something Mary would be capable of, to love him for himself alone,' said Desmond rather as though he were quoting, as perhaps he was, 'Without any hope of return.'

'Now that's something I should like to see,' said Maitland, getting to his feet. 'No, don't move, we needn't leave yet. I was just going to ask Jenny to warm up the coffee pot, mine's gone cold. And is this the only surprise you had for me, or is there something more tucked up your sleeve?'

'Nothing else,' said Desmond shaking his head, which Antony was beginning to think was a habit of his. 'I think myself we've quite enough to contend with as it is.'

'Coke said they didn't have a living-in servant. Ought we to see the 'daily'?'

'I already did, and she's no use to us. Never there in the evening, for one thing. And she must have got some inkling from my questions that something was badly amiss, beyond the fact that Elizabeth had taken herself off to an hotel. But all I could get out of her was that all men are beasts . . . which isn't exactly helpful in the circumstances, is it?'

II

Owen Barrie's house was in a street not far from Kempenfeldt Square, and viewed from outside was not unlike Sir Nicholas's home. Once inside however, the differences became immediately apparent. Here was none of the comfortable shabbiness of Number Five, everything

38

was modern, quite out of keeping with the period of the building, and not only modern but quite new. An ostentatious display of wealth, thought Maitland to himself, following Desmond Barleycorn into a room designated by what was obviously a charlady of the more independent type as 'the study'. But he revived his opinion a little when their host rose to greet them from one of the leather chairs near the fireplace. Owen Barrie had an air about him very far from ostentation and a kindliness of manner that made the two younger men feel at home in spite of the rather embarrassing nature of their errand. Antony was immediately reminded of his friend Detective Chief Inspector Sykes; there was the same north country accent, slurred over now by years of living away from his native heath, the same manner at once forthright and friendly. And at the same time he was recalling that the refrigerator in his own kitchen was a Barrie-Mode. It had seen years of service so the replacement couldn't be high. Perhaps the original profit had been, in any case there was every evidence that the manufacture of kitchen appliances was a profitable one.

'Well now,' said Barrie waving invitingly towards chairs. Antony himself would have given the world to be free to roam about the room as they talked, but on such short acquaintance that was obviously not a good idea. He sat down therefore and looked across at Owen. 'This is a nasty business you've come to see me about,' said Barrie bluntly, 'and you two working on the wrong side of the fence.'

'There's no question about calling you as a witness,' said Desmond quickly. 'At least, not as far as I know,' he added cautiously. But both Mr Maitland and I felt it might be helpful if we had a talk.'

'This is Mr Maitland, is it?' There could be no doubt where Barrie's main interest lay. 'I've heard of you,' he added, and the word sounded to Antony's ears like an accusation. 'But I always thought you'd be the kind of chap I'd like to see in my corner. What are you doing mixing yourself up with a fellow like Coke?'

'He's my client,' said Antony mildly.

'So he may be, but –'

'It was Edward the last time you spoke of him,' said Desmond, interrupting again, so that Antony realised for the first time the full depth of his concern for his partner. 'Can you really believe this story that's going round about him?'

'I can believe what my own son told me, can't I? Besides, there's Elizabeth. An angel out of heaven she is, not one to tell lies, and what it must have cost her to have to come out with all this is beyond my imagining.'

'Distressing certainly,' said Maitland taking over again. He wasn't quite sure where Desmond's obvious partisanship would land them. 'But may I remind you, Mr Barrie, that the matter is still *sub judice.* For some reason the libel action will be heard very quickly, but until the court has reached a decision –'

'Before the divorce?' Barrie sounded taken aback. 'I didn't think husband and wife could sue each other,' he said, 'and that it was only because they'd be divorced by then that the fellow was able to take Elizabeth to court.'

'That isn't the case any longer. I admit the court has still some discretion in the matter – the phrase is "if it appears that no substantial benefit would accrue to either party", isn't it, Desmond? – but in a case as serious as this I think there's no question of any interference.'

'Oh, I see. In the circumstances, you know,' said Owen Barrie confidentially, 'I can't for the life of me think why Coke should want to dispute the matter. If he hadn't done that –'

'Mrs Coke would still have had to wait until they had been married for three years before presenting her petition.'

'Yes, I know all about that. I said to her myself, six months isn't such a very long time, but I think she was quite desperate, poor child, and couldn't consider waiting.'

'My client says he offered her an immediate separation and an allowance.'

'That may be true,' said Owen grudgingly, 'but it wasn't what she wanted. He's got this pig-headed notion about divorce, at the end of the six months she'd still have been just where she is today.'

'You agree with her action then?'

'She must be free,' said Barrie firmly. 'Poor child, when she told me –'

'She told you?' said Maitland, forgetting for the moment to maintain a professional imperturbability.

'Of course she did, in this very room. It was an ordeal for both of us, I'm sure you can understand that, but when she explained I saw it was the only thing to do if she was to be really free. And no use waiting, as I said, since Coke has this idea in his head that he doesn't agree with divorce.'

'According to Mrs Coke's story he has some ideas that are considerably more bizarre.'

'There's no accounting for that sort of thing. And I'll tell you straight, if it weren't for Elizabeth I could almost sympathise with him. Everything straightforward, that's my motto, but people get these queer ideas and perhaps they can't help it.'

'And it was after your conversation with Mrs Coke,' said Maitland, 'that you spoke to your son about the matter?'

'What do you think? Of course I talked to him about it. And I'm not saying, mind you, that David is everything I could wish him to be, in fact if you want to know what I think,' said Owen Barrie, suddenly confidential, 'it will be clogs to clogs in three generations, just like they say where I come from. Never done a hand's turn in his life so far as I know, and has all those la-di-da notions.' He paused,

41

eyeing his two visitors doubtfully. 'But they won't seem so strange to you, I dare say.'

'I'm more interested,' said Maitland frankly, 'in understanding his part in all this.'

'Love, he says,' replied Owen promptly. 'But if you want to know what I call it, Mr Maitland, it's plain old fashioned lust. He wanted her and she didn't want him, not that way, though she says she likes him well enough. And that was the only way he could get her. So he went along with Coke's foul ideas.'

'It certainly seems that love is not quite the right word,' said Maitland dryly. 'Did Mrs Coke explain to you why she consented?'

'Because she was afraid of her husband, that's why. Still is for that matter. As for him, if that's the way he gets his amusement he doesn't need a divorce, does he? Get himself what he wants by paying for it, isn't that the way nowadays? Unless of course,' he added thoughtfully, 'it's more titillating when his wife's concerned.'

'That might be the case, I suppose.'

Something in Antony's tone alerted Owen Barrie. 'Don't you believe me then?' he asked belligerently.

'I'm sure you believe the story, Mr Barrie,' said Maitland pacifically.

'That's nothing to the point. Elizabeth wouldn't lie,' he said again, 'and as for David . . . well, I did my best to bring him up right, but I seem to have got off wrong somewhere. His mother dying, that's probably what did it. I'd say he's got the morals of a billy-goat, but he wouldn't be lying about a matter like this, because what would it gain him?'

'I've been wondering about that myself.'

'Well the answer is, nothing, nothing at all.'

'You did say, Mr Barrie, that Mrs Coke had to be free. What did you mean by that?'

'Just what I said, young man.'

42

Maitland had a private smile for the phrase. Any moment now the other man would be lapsing into his native dialect. 'I was wondering, you see, whether perhaps there had been some inducement offered to him, if Mrs Coke had promised to marry him for instance, after she got her divorce?'

The friendly attitude with which the interview had started had been wearing thin for some time now, and Antony was frankly expecting that this question would bring an outburst of wrath. To his surprise, however, Barrie gazed at him for a moment open mouthed and then burst out laughing. There was no doubt about the genuineness of his amusement. 'That's a good one, that is,' he said.

'Are you going to explain that, Mr Barrie?'

For a moment Owen hesitated. 'Elizabeth did make me promise not to say anything,' he said doubtfully after a moment, 'but it was their friends she meant, and I think she'd see you ought to know, then perhaps you'll stop doubting David's word. There's no question of her marrying him. Once she's got her divorce, when she's wiped the floor with that fellow, and with you two as well, though I've nothing against you, either of you, she's promised to marry me.'

III

It was customary for the Maitlands to lunch downstairs on Saturdays, and Jenny had been charged with the task of making Antony's excuses. She had however promised to leave soup and sandwiches for her husband and his companion, and they walked back to Kempenfeldt Square when they left Owen Barrie's house. Desmond was rather silent on the way, and it wasn't until the soup had been placed on the low light and they were relaxing together

43

with a drink that he spoke his mind. 'You were leading up to that admission of his all the time, weren't you?' he asked.

'That he was engaged to Elizabeth Coke, insofar as one can be engaged to someone who is still married? Yes, the possibility had occurred to me.'

'I don't see your line of reasoning, I'm afraid.'

'If it's any comfort to you it's gone a long way towards convincing me that you're right about our client,' Antony informed him.

'Yes, I'm glad about that, but I still want to know –'

'It's not too easy to explain.' But Antony resigned himself to trying to do so. 'The first thing was Aunt Harriet . . . does Elizabeth Coke have any relations of her own by the way?'

'Not a soul, as far as I know. The old lady was Edward's aunt, well I suppose his aunt by marriage since her name was Coke too.'

'Yes but I thought then, and what you've told me since about Elizabeth confirms the idea, that it was an odd sort of job for her to have. She doesn't sound the ministering angel type. Only then I wondered, as the old lady is so wealthy, perhaps she had an eye to the main chance. Old ladies have been known to leave their attendants quite comfortably off. And if I was right about that of course it must have seemed quite providential to her when Edward Coke came along. She may not have had much taste for marriage but it would be infinitely better than being at the beck and call of an old woman, and she probably thought – as I think Coke himself did – that Aunt Harriet would make him her heir.'

'It still seems a little far-fetched,' said Desmond slowly.

'Yes, but wait a bit. Aunt Harriet died – when was it Coke said? – last November I believe. And it was just about six months ago that David Barrie started visiting the Cokes without waiting for an invitation that included his father. You said something, didn't you, about his possibly telling the truth about being in love with Elizabeth? My idea is

44

that she induced him to back up her story by promising to marry him.'

'But his father says –'

'Yes, and I think he believes it. He said Elizabeth swore him to secrecy, didn't he? She'll have given him a good reason for that, that it isn't proper to be talking about remarrying until the divorce is final. If she can keep David hoodwinked until he has given the evidence she wants, she'll be home and dry.'

'Yes, I see what you mean, and what Owen Barrie told us about her actually having promised to marry him tends to confirm the first part of this idea, doesn't it? She married Edward in expectation of plenty, but when Aunt Harriet's money went elsewhere she thought a wealthy manu- facturer would be preferable to her moderately well-off solicitor.'

'Yes, that's the point I was leading to, Desmond. Do you see now why it reinforces my belief?'

'Yes I do. And I don't blame you for doubting him,' he added generously. 'After all you don't know Edward as I do.'

'The trouble is I don't see my way clear. Do you suppose any of these people we're going to see can give us a lead?'

'I don't know, but I have heard you're awfully good at putting two and two together,' said Desmond diffidently. He had realised already that there were certain subjects on which Maitland was sensitive. 'Anyway, we'll feel we've done our best,' he added, and unwittingly put his finger on another sore point.

'Indeed we shall,' said Maitland, heaving himself out of his chair and nobly refraining from making a snappish reply. 'Finish your drink,' he said, 'while I look at the soup. Who is our first appointment this afternoon, by the way?'

'Primrose Ross, and if you want to know why,' said Desmond smiling up at his host, 'it's because I want to get it

45

over with. She isn't one of my favourite people.'

IV

This time they took Desmond's car, which had been parked
outside Number Five Kempenfeldt Square ever since he
arrived that morning. 'If we find a place to leave her,' said
Desmond, pulling smoothly away from the curb, 'we can
walk round from Primrose's to both the Walpoles and the
Stowes. They all live more or less in the Bayswater area.
Then if it isn't too late we can phone Mary Jerrold and ask
her to meet us for a drink somewhere. She's one of those
eccentric people who like living in the city, so it would be
quite convenient for her.'

'That sounds an excellent programme,' said Antony, set-
tling himself more comfortably in his place, and was
reminded as he always was when he watched someone
else take the controls of the injury to his shoulder that
prevented him from driving himself. The reminder also
brought consciousness of the ever present ache there, that
sometimes he could forget for an hour or two at a time.
But that was something never to be mentioned, even to
Jenny. Someone had once had the temerity to suggest that
he should have a car with special controls, and been well
snubbed for their pains; not realising that it was the circumstances of the injury, and not the injury itself that
caused the most pain. To distract himself he asked idly
now, 'What's wrong with Miss Ross? Why isn't she your
favourite person?'

'She's a bit of a drip,' said Desmond inelegantly. 'To tell
you the truth I could never understand her friendship with
Elizabeth. No, that's not quite accurate ... I could understand Primrose doting on her friend, but not the other way
round.'

46

'Why do you think Mrs Coke wrote that letter?'

'Ignorance of the law for one thing,' said Desmond rather severely. 'I think – but I admit I'm guessing – that she'd heard about privileged communications, and thought because this was part of her case it would be covered too. And I think she was just so pleased with herself to be able to put over a fast one on Edward that she had to tell someone.'

'And why did Miss Ross divulge the contents? Are you sure it wasn't spite?'

'You wait till you see her,' Desmond prophesied. 'You'll understand what I mean then.'

Miss Ross had a tiny flat in an expensive block, so that Antony wasn't sure whether its smallness was due to convenience or economy. She was rather too tall and rather too thin, though not ill-looking, and she greeted them with the remark that she hadn't the faintest idea why they should wish to see her. 'Not that it isn't very nice of you to call, Desmond,' she said, 'and to bring Mr Maitland with you. But I'm Elizabeth's friend, you know, and it isn't likely I'd do anything to help you when I think what . . . what agony that awful man has put her through.'

'What interests me, Miss Ross,' said Antony, 'is that you know Mrs Coke so well I'm sure you can help us.'

'But I don't really want to help you,' she said petulantly.

'That isn't really the point.' He glanced at Desmond, who took up the explanation perhaps a little over-patiently.

'You have received, I believe, a *subpoena* to give evidence in the libel suit Coke *versus* Coke.'

'If you mean that bit of paper, it came yesterday.'

'A rather important bit of paper,' said Desmond. 'We have to prove that the libel was published – '

'It was a private letter!'

'I'm afraid that in law that constitutes publication, especially as the contents were communicated to other

47

people. There is also the question of proving damage.'

'I don't understand these legal things. What do you mean, proving damage?'

'Proving that Edward suffered from the story that had been spread about him, both professionally and in his reputation.'

'You mean to say he wants money from Elizabeth? Is that what all this is about, his idea of revenge?'

'No, that isn't what he wants at all. He's bringing the action purely in self-defence, Elizabeth really left him no other option, but without the proof of damage I spoke of, an action wouldn't lie.'

'Oh, that's just too much!' If Primrose wasn't Desmond's favourite woman, obviously he wasn't her ideal man either. 'I don't wish to seem inhospitable, Mr Maitland, but I do wish you'd both go away and leave me alone.'

'We will, of course, if that's what you want,' said Antony. His reasonable tone was a very fair copy of Desmond's. 'But do you understand we shall need your evidence in court, and it might be easier for you if we prepared you a little for the kind of questions you'll be asked?'

'Is that the law too?' It occurred to Antony that she might very well be about to add, the law is an ass, but she contented herself saying grudgingly, when he answered her question with a nod, 'Oh, very well, I suppose I'd better talk to you then. And we'd better all sit down.'

The little room was almost suffocatingly hot, and so small they all seemed to be crowded together. Antony thought wryly that even if he had given way to the impulse for movement there would have been nowhere to go, he was almost knee-to-knee with Primrose Ross. 'First, I'd like to know how long you've known Elizabeth Coke,' he said.

'Just since her marriage. You don't know her, Mr Maitland, or you wouldn't be trying to do this to her. I

48

knew from the moment I saw her we were going to be friends. She's – she's such a lady.'

'Yes, I'm sure. Everything I've heard confirms that,' said Antony, and did not add, on the surface at any rate. 'You had known Edward Coke for longer than that, then?'

'Our parents were friends, but it was only after he married Elizabeth that I visited them at all frequently. Before that, when my father was alive, there'd be occasional dinner parties. But I was asked to the wedding, and Elizabeth and I naturally took to each other.'

'And after that you were in her confidence?'

'We talked about everything.'

'About her relations with her husband?'

'Not that, of course.' The question obviously affronted her. 'One doesn't talk about things like that, whatever you men may do among yourselves.'

'No hint at all of trouble between them?'

'She did say once that Edward was rather a cold man,' said Primrose reluctantly.

'Did she elaborate at all?'

'Of course she didn't, and I didn't ask.'

'Then this famous letter, when it came, must have been something of a shock to you.'

'Oh, it was!'

'The sort of thing perhaps that you wouldn't expect one lady to write to another,' Maitland suggested.

'Not in the ordinary way, no,' Primrose agreed. 'But in the circumstances ... it was the cry of an overwrought soul,' she added with dignity.

'Yes, I see.' He was aware that Desmond was trying to catch his eye, but that was the last thing he wanted. 'We've both read the letter, Miss Ross, and I don't want to upset you by going into details at this stage, but I must warn you that it will be read in court, and you will be asked some questions about it both by myself and by Elizabeth Coke's counsel.'

'If the law says I must answer I shall do so to the best of my ability. In fact, Mr Maitland, I shall be only too pleased for everyone to know exactly how wicked Edward is.'

'That's the opinion you reached when you read the letter?'

'How could I think anything else?'

'You weren't at all shocked that Mrs Coke should have confided in you, an unmarried lady, in this way?'

'Certainly not. I have said that there are many occasions that override the conventions, and this was one of them. It would have been much more improper for Elizabeth to speak of this dreadful thing . . . to a man for instance.'

Again Antony suppressed the temptation to meet his colleague's eye. 'Yet you yourself disclosed the contents of the letter,' he said.

'Because it was only common justice that everyone should know exactly what Edward is like. There he's been all these years, going to church, pretending to be better than everyone else. And I felt Elizabeth deserved some sympathy too, and that her friends should know she's suffered.'

'I see.' Desmond was right, he thought, there was no malicious intent here, except towards Edward Coke. 'But you admit, Miss Ross,' he said, 'that you have no previous knowledge of any difficulties between Elizabeth Coke and her husband.'

'That's quite true.'

'There were two couples, I believe, to whom you spoke of the letter?'

'Yes, the Walpoles and the Stowes. I felt it only right –' she began again.

'Yes, quite so. You didn't mention it to either of the Barries, for instance?'

50

'To David Barrie, certainly not. I consider him almost equally to blame with Edward, what that poor girl must have suffered!'

'Not to David Barrie perhaps, but you know his father as well.'

'Certainly I do, but a matter that concerned so close a relation ... even if I'd thought it proper to mention the matter to a man.'

'You don't think much of us, do you?' Again Maitland's look was humorous but it brought no answering spark. 'The two couples you spoke of, in each case a man was involved.'

'That's quite different. I spoke to Fran alone over a cup of tea in the afternoon. And I made Joanna take me somewhere alone, I couldn't have faced Terence with the story. But I told each of them particularly to tell their husbands, because it was a thing I felt they should know about Edward, whom they seemed to consider as a friend.'

'As you did yourself, Miss Ross, unless I'm very much mistaken.'

'The husband of a friend,' she corrected him. 'He wasn't good enough for her, though I dare say nobody could be, but I didn't know then he was such a hypocrite.'

'And that,' said Antony as they left five minutes later, 'is about as kind a word as anyone is going to be able to find for our client if we can't put a stop to this somehow.'

'Do you think we can?'

'I wouldn't give you odds at the moment. And I'll tell you something Desmond, I don't think much of our chances when my uncle has finished with the lady we've just left. She's so convinced now that Coke is a villain that by the time the matter gets into court a hundred things may have occurred to her to confirm that assessment.'

He stopped for a moment dead in his tracks. 'Did you say we'd leave the car here?' he asked vaguely. 'I don't know this area very well and I wouldn't give tuppence for my chances of finding it again.'

'I think I can manage,' said Desmond. 'It will only take us about ten minutes to reach the Walpoles.'

V

The Walpoles' home would come, Antony thought, under the frightful category that the estate agents know as a maisonette. It was the upper half of an old house that had been divided to provide the tenants with as much privacy as possible and it was a choice address as the windows of the big room to which they were shown overlooked the park. Mrs Walpole had let them in, a small slight woman whose dark hair managed to be both straight and bouncy. This, in a way, matched her manner. She was only too conscious of the seriousness of the matter in hand, but she was naturally a cheerful soul and couldn't altogether hide it. And when she introduced her husband he was just such another. A good deal taller than his wife, not wanting to betray any insensibility, but always conscious of the basic rightness of things. He was – Maitland had been studying his brief in the meantime – a Chartered Accountant, and Frances, whom he could well imagine being efficient, sometimes went down to his office to help him.

'But only because I want to,' she assured him, 'because we like being together. We've been married eight years and no sign of a family yet, so I don't suppose we're going to have one now.'

Antony allowed himself the brief, but not altogether amused thought that he had received more unsolicited confidences since this matter began than in the past five years, and though this wasn't altogether true it gave him an added dislike for Edward Coke's affairs. Still the Walpoles looked a nice couple, and if anything interesting came of their talk –.

Roland may have been watching his expression. He said now, amiably, 'Mr Maitland doesn't want to hear about us, Fran. He and Desmond want to talk about Edward's affairs.'

'Well, I know that of course,' she retorted. 'And I want to tell you right away that it's all nonsense. We don't believe a word of it.'

'You're going to have to elaborate that for us, Mrs Walpole. A word of what?'

'Sit down first,' said Roland, who seemed to have a good grasp of essentials. When they had done so he went on, 'I've been looking this libel business up and trying to explain it to Fran, but I don't think women have legal minds, do you?'

'My aunt wouldn't agree with you,' Maitland told him. 'She was a barrister on the West Midland circuit until she married my uncle two years ago.' He smiled at Frances. 'Still, I'll admit she may be an exception.'

'Well, it all seems very stupid to me,' said Frances in a downright way. 'You've got to prove damage, though that isn't what Edward wants at all. All he wants is to clear his good name.'

'And what if he can't?'

'It will break him professionally but he'll still have his friends,' said Roland.

'You're both convinced that there was a libel published then –'

'Well of course there was, I saw it,' said Fran positively.

'– and that the defence of truth would not be a valid one?'

'Yes.' Roland took a moment to smile at his wife and then looked back at Maitland. 'And again I have to tell you you'll be walking into trouble in court if you try to get some logical reasons out of Fran. It's all pure instinct with her.

We've known Edward for years and though we neither of us dislike Elizabeth, if their stories are in flat contradiction . . . she couldn't possibly believe such a thing about him.'   'But with you, Mr Walpole, it's different?'

'I suppose I must be honest, not altogether. My first instinct when Fran told me about the letter Primrose had showed her was one of complete disbelief. But thinking it out I believe I can justify that with a little logic. Edward's attitude is consistent with everything we know of him. He's nothing to gain, except the feeling that he's doing the right thing in refusing her a divorce. Elizabeth seems to want freedom, therefore you might say a motive exists for accusing him in this way.'

'I've got a feeling there's a fallacy there somewhere,' said Antony thoughtfully. 'However, it's a point of view I want very badly to get over and I'm grateful for your help. Did you know Mrs Coke before her marriage?'

'Not to say know, though we'd visited old Mrs Coke sometimes, and seen her there.'

'What was your impression of her?'

'She was very self-effacing. Wouldn't you say that was true, Fran?'

'She was all over the old lady,' said Fran mutinously.

'Come now, my dear, you're being wise after the event. And you can't deny we were both pleased when we knew they were going to be married. Edward is such a good chap, and it's no fun growing into middle age alone.'

'Did either of them ever speak to you about their relationship after they were married?'

'No, of course not. Edward wouldn't under any circumstances, and though I believe that women are sometimes more outspoken on personal matters, at least in the company of their own sex, Fran and Elizabeth were never close in that way.'

'Is that right, Mrs Walpole?'

'Quite right. Edward is the nicest man, a bit of a puritan perhaps –'

'Now that is something that could be open to misconstruction,' Antony told her. 'Any hint of repressed emotions would convey exactly the opposite impression to the one we want.'

'Yes, of course I see that. But actually that wasn't what I meant at all.'

'Tell me,' said Maitland encouragingly.

'It's a matter of believing, really and truly believing. But I didn't mean to imply that he was puritan in the sense that he couldn't see a joke. He really has a very strong sense of humour.'

'Perhaps the jury will regard that as a sign of grace,' said Maitland lightly, and caught Roland's eye and exchanged a smile with him. 'You can help us prove that the libel was published, but in your eyes at least it did my client no harm. Will you tell me exactly what happened when Miss Ross came to you with Mrs Coke's letter?'

'I didn't see her,' said Roland. 'Fran had better tell you.'

'I wasn't at the office that day,' said Fran, 'and she came to tea. She often does that when I have a free afternoon, and naturally would be glad enough to be by myself, but I don't know how she knows I'll be here. Roland and I have a joke that she has a crystal ball. Anyway, she came and she followed me into the kitchen while I waited for the kettle to boil, and it was perfectly obvious that she was bursting with information of some sort. So I didn't bother to carry the tray through, just sat down opposite her at the table when everything was ready, and "What do you think of that?" she asked me, and pushed that horrible letter across the table.'

'And what *did* you think of it, Mrs Walpole?'

'I've already told you, that it was a tissue of lies from beginning to end.'

It wasn't only speaking in quotation marks, there were clichés as well, thought Maitland ruefully. But he like these two and his appreciation of the defence of their friend was not entirely professional. 'Did you tell Miss Ross that?' he asked.

'Yes, of course I did. And to tell you the truth, – I know it's silly – but I pushed the letter back to her and went to the sink to wash my hands. I felt as if they were dirty. And Primrose was stuffing the sheets of papers back into her handbag and saying quite complacently, "I thought it was something you ought to know".'

'What did you say to that?'

'Of course I challenged her, did she believe it? But quite obviously she did and all I could get out of her was, Elizabeth was such a pure person it must have been particularly horrible for her.'

'So that evening you told your husband?'

'I nearly didn't,' said Fran, 'I could hardly bring myself to say a thing like that. Only it was quite obvious that Primrose wasn't going to stop with me in showing round the letter, and I thought Roland had better hear it first before it came back to him from anyone else. And he was just as horrified and just as disbelieving as I was, and I think he'd have been a lot ruder to Primrose if she'd been there then.'

'Yes, I dare say I should,' Roland Walpole agreed. 'We talked it over, of course, and then agreed to try to forget the whole thing. Elizabeth had left Edward and whether she got her divorce or not, knowing him, he was likely to live as a bachelor for the rest of his life. As far as we were concerned, the least said soonest mended.'

'I wish more people would take that attitude about others' affairs,' said Maitland. 'But the thing that intrigues me is this . . . do you know the Barries?'

'Oh yes, quite well.'

56

'Then tell me what you think of David Barrie.'

'It's a little awkward. Owen Barrie was a friend of my father's, though rather younger than he was. I don't want –'

'Off the record, if you like.'

Roland looked at him for a long moment. 'Does that mean you won't question me about this in court?'

'I won't, but I can't guarantee what Mrs Coke's counsel may or may not ask you,' said Antony honestly.

'Then I may as well commit myself. He's a queer piece of work whichever way you look at him, and as far as he's concerned Elizabeth's story isn't unbelievable.'

'Had you any clue that he might be in love with her?'

'No, but that much might be true. What about you, Fran?'

'I did wonder once or twice, and then I thought I was imagining things. Elizabeth always seems so – so demure,' she said.

'And yet you say you disbelieved her story straight away.'

'We knew Edward you see,' said Fran as though that was sufficient answer.

'About their relationship – Edward and Elizabeth Coke. Had you ever had any clue that she might be afraid of him?'

'No, and I don't believe it for a moment, it's absolutely ridiculous.'

'To return to David, somebody said he had the morals of a billygoat.'

'That would fit him well enough I think,' said Roland judiciously, but then he smiled. 'Very well in fact,' he added.

'What I'm wondering you see ... he wouldn't be too worried by the publication of this story?'

'To tell you the truth I've an idea he'd think it a good joke,' said Roland in a tone of disgust.

'Then I think that's all.' Maitland got up a little reluctantly. 'I won't forget my promise to you, Mr Walpole, and I won't ask Mrs Walpole any awkward questions about David Barrie either.'

'I wish I could see how our evidence could help Edward,' said Roland.

'I think mainly as to his character. Your confidence in him may impress the court. But it isn't enough,' he added ruefully to Desmond as they let themselves out into the street. 'The jury will just think they're too nice a couple to believe badly of anybody.'

'You're being illogical yourself now,' Desmond pointed out. 'In this case whichever side you take you've got to believe ill of somebody.'

'That's true,' said Antony sighing. He was moving a little stiffly as he often did when he was tired, and Desmond gave him a curious look but fortunately had the sense to refrain from comment.

'Let's see if we have any better luck with Terence and Joanna,' he said hopefully.

VI

The Stowes were a tall couple and as soon as he saw the husband Antony was reminded at once of his client, though here was the animation that was lacking in Edward Coke. There were, however, the same almost classical good looks, and turning to appraise Joanna Stowe he was aware of surprise. She looked somehow out of place in the circle in which Edward Coke and his wife seemed to have been moving. Not that she was at all bad-looking, her face was rather thin but she had a pale, clear complexion. Her hair, however, was cut in an old-fashioned bob, straight and rather straggly, obviously she had done nothing at all to assist nature. And she wore a rather faded print frock, which might have been sensible if she'd just been about to

58

start on her household chores, but on a Saturday afternoon in London, in a flat that – while it didn't have the opulence of the Barrie residence – was obviously not that of a pauper, it looked singularly out of place. Terence Stowe (again he cast his mind back to his brief) was a surgeon at one of the big London hospitals, while his wife did volunteer work at a children's day centre, travelling some distance into the suburbs to do so.

They were welcomed pleasantly enough, a little fussily in fact on Joanna's part, but there was an underlying coldness in the air, and Antony wasn't surprised when Terence Stowe said abruptly, almost as though the words were an accusation, 'You're on Edward's side.'

'He's our client certainly,' said Antony mildly.

'Well, I can understand Desmond, he's Edward's junior partner and has to do what he says. But I always understood a barrister had the option of picking and choosing in civil cases, I can't say I admire your choice of cause, Mr Maitland.'

'That's a matter of opinion, after all.'

'If you knew Elizabeth –' Joanna began.

'Mr Barleycorn does know her,' Antony pointed out. 'May we get straight to the point? I should very much like to know exactly what happened when Miss Primrose Ross showed you Mrs Coke's letter.'

'That's your story, darling,' said Terence sitting back in his chair.

Joanna grimaced as though she found the subject disagreeable, but started willingly enough. 'She rang me up. Primrose did I mean. She said Elizabeth and Edward had broken up and it was all Edward's fault and she felt all their friends ought to know it in fairness to Elizabeth. I'm not at home during the day – she called at breakfast time – so I told her to come round that evening, and when she did and I let her in she wouldn't let me come back in here where Terence was. "I couldn't repeat such things in front of him," she said. So we went into the kitchen and she showed me the letter. I was horrified, of course, but I said at once that Terence ought to know about it. She was a bit unwilling but he came back in here with me, and he read the letter too. And I could tell his reaction was just the same as mine because he said at once, "Where is Elizabeth staying?" '

'It was a stupid question,' said Terence, 'because the name of the hotel was at the top of the letter. Primrose said she'd phoned there and offered Elizabeth somewhere to stay, but Elizabeth said she'd rather be alone. If you've seen Primrose's place you'll not be surprised at that, they'd have been right on top of each other, quite unbearable. So I told Joanna to ring her later – I mean I told her this after Primrose had gone – and see if she'd like to stay with us. But she maintained she was quite all right and said again that she wanted to think things out.'

'How long have you known Mrs Coke?'

'Since the wedding,' said Joanna, looking at Terence who nodded. 'She's a lovely person.'

'And how long have you known Edward Coke?'

'Terence has known him pretty well all his life, and I've known him since we were married. That's ten years ago.'

'Have you ever considered him the sort of man who would treat his wife in this way?'

It was Terence who answered him. 'Naturally we haven't, it isn't the sort of thing that comes to your mind about your friends. But in your profession as well as mine you must know, Mr Maitland, that where human nature is concerned practically anything can happen, and I have to tell you that it seemed far more likely that Edward was abnormal in this one way at least than that Elizabeth had concocted such a story. Besides her letter said quite clearly that she had David Barrie's backing, and the story isn't exactly creditable to him.' 'I've been told,' said Maitland vaguely, 'that the publicity might not worry him. He might regard the whole thing as a joke.'

'Anyone would be worried about a thing like that,' said Joanna firmly. 'David is rather – rather a dilettante.' She produced the word as though she was proud of it. 'But I don't think that even he would consent to such a story unless it was true.'

'All the same, you based your belief in it on Mrs Coke's character, not his?' He was watching Terence Stowe as he spoke, and saw his quick frown. A moment later he was smiling.

'David is very much a law unto himself,' he said. 'You can appreciate that, though I think it's a bit beyond Joanna.'

'I don't know why you should say that,' she said, and the phrase came into Antony's mind, ruffling her feathers angrily. I'm getting as bad as this lot, he thought to himself, but kept his amusement to himself.

'Because you're a woman, my dear,' said Terence easily. 'But being the man he is I don't think his part in all this is really difficult of explanation. He agreed to Edward's rather bizarre request because he was in love with Elizabeth and that was the only way he could get her. Similarly, he agreed to back up her story for the same reason.'

'It doesn't sound very much like love to me, to force yourself on an unwilling woman,' Antony told him.

Terence frowned again, but Joanna forestalled eagerly any reply he might have been about to make. 'We must be fair to David,' she said. 'I don't suppose he realised she was unwilling. She was so much afraid of Edward –'

'Sufficiently afraid of him to pretend a compliance she didn't feel?'

'Well she must have, mustn't she?'

'That isn't the answer Mr Maitland wants, Joanna,' her

husband broke in. 'Tell him what Elizabeth told you when you phoned her at the hotel.'

'Well, she said the marriage had never been consummated, but that Edward had treated her right from the beginning as something that belonged to him, a mere *thing*,' said Joanna with emphasis. 'I think he probably knocked her about, but she'd never admit to that, of course.'

'Now there,' said Terence, 'I think you're being unjust to our friend.'

'He's no friend of mine,' said Joanna firmly.

'Nor of mine now. All the same, there are more subtle ways of terrorising someone in your power than mere physical abuse. Even you, Desmond, will agree that Edward isn't altogether a simple character.'

'Which of us is?' said Maitland lightly before his companion could reply. He was increasingly conscious of Barleycorn's uneasiness at the way the conversation was going. 'This wasn't mentioned in the letter, but are you telling me now that Mrs Coke claims to have been a virgin until her encounters with David Barrie?'

'She says she was a virgin when she married Coke, which in the circumstances comes to the same thing. And no proof either way to be had, Desmond,' he added, allowing his amusement to show for the moment. 'If she were *virgo intacta* before, she certainly wasn't after the encounters with David.'

'Which I don't believe ever took place,' said Desmond hotly, unable to contain himself any longer.

'That, as your colleague pointed out a moment ago, is a matter of opinion,' said Terence. 'Yours, I believe, is coloured by the relationship in which you stand to Edward professionally. Surely our opinion is a little less biased.'

'And so, believing this story,' said Maitland hastily, 'you passed it on to some of your other friends.'

'To one or two people. I've already given Desmond their names and addresses.'

'Yes, we shall see them if necessary,' Maitland assured him. 'But it seems we've got everything we need in this connection already.'

'Hatred, ridicule and contempt,' said Stowe thoughtfully. 'But, you know, I don't think you've a leg to stand on in trying to prove that what Elizabeth says isn't true. And I must say I for one am glad of it. If ever a woman did, she deserves her divorce.'

'If we must be exact,' said Joanna, who had been simmering quietly in the background during this last discussion, 'it was I who did the passing on. I thought it only fair to Elizabeth.'

'Yes, I see. That seems to be all we can do here then,' he added, glancing at Desmond and coming to his feet.

'Just a moment.' Terence Stowe spoke hurriedly. 'There's one thing you ought to know and that Desmond may have omitted to tell you.'

'Oh?'

'If Elizabeth hadn't been desperate, if she'd felt able to wait another six months for her divorce, she needn't have gone into this whole unpleasant business at all.'

'Now you do surprise me, Mr Stowe.'

'She would have been able to establish the irretrievable breakdown of the marriage by proving Edward's adultery with one of his staff.'

Maitland was still standing and Desmond Barleycorn had risen too. Without looking he put out a hand now and rested it on his colleague's arm, he had a feeling that the young man was not too far from an explosion. 'Come now, Mr Stowe,' he said in a rallying tone, 'you can't have it both ways. Either Edward Coke is a cold fish, who can't even be troubled to make love to his own wife, or – or he isn't,' he concluded lamely.

The protest may not have been well expressed but it certainly conveyed his meaning. 'That's something I hadn't thought of,' said Terence slowly. 'All the same, Joanna will tell you that Elizabeth had her doubts about his relationship with this girl, Mary Jerrold, and to my mind that proves how desperate poor Elizabeth was.' He was speaking firmly but for a moment Maitland thought almost at random.

They left after that with due politeness on both sides and walked back to the place where Desmond's car was parked outside the block of flats where Primrose Ross lived. 'I know that was an ordeal for you, Desmond,' said Antony sympathetically as they went, 'but for a while they annoyed me just as much.'

'Only for a while?'

'Well, to tell you the truth I began to have my doubts as to how much they really believe of what they're saying. It's probably all imagination,' he added and shrugged, and then glanced at his watch. 'Is it too late to see Miss Jerrold?'

'There's a box across the road and I'll call her from there,' said Desmond. 'And if you want to know what I think, a drink is just what we need.'

VII

Miss Jerrold was agreeable and arrived at the appointed meeting place, a pub suggested by Maitland, only a few minutes after the two men got there. It was still not long after opening time and for a while they had the place to themselves.

Mary was a pretty girl with a mass of mouse-coloured hair and the gentle manner that Antony had heard described so often when Elizabeth Coke was being spoken of. Perhaps Edward really was attracted to her, perhaps she was his type, but as their conversation progressed he began to form the opinion that in this case at least there was no deceit about it. She was genuinely self-effacing – perhaps a little too much so for his own taste – and certainly there was no doubting her genuine affection for her employer.

She only waited for the introductions to be effected, to greet Maitland politely with the words, 'I'm so glad you're helping Edward,' before she turned to Desmond and asked eagerly, 'Have you been able to find out anything, just what are his chances?'

Desmond began to look hunted and threw a despairing look at his companion. 'We're ... proceeding with our enquiries,' he said cautiously.

'Oh, don't be silly, Desmond, you sound just like a policeman. I really want to know –'

'Don't blame him, Miss Jerrold. Even though you work in the same office he's bound to be discreet about this, as you know. I can just tell you that we've heard a lot of opinion and very little fact. But in the long run some of it may be of help.' He hadn't really very much hope on that score but it seemed unkind to say anything else.

'I know exactly what you mean,' said Mary. 'Nothing was any good at all.' He was to discover as he knew her better that she had two personalities: the professional one in which she could see as far through a brick wall as the next man, and another very feminine one.

'I'm afraid that's true,' he admitted ruefully. 'However –'

'There wasn't anything else he could do, you do understand that, Mr Maitland,' she said earnestly. 'Once this dreadful allegation was made he had to bring the libel suit, otherwise he would have seemed to be admitting it. And at least he'll have his day in court, be able to deny it. And I suppose a few people will believe him,' she added sadly.

'You do, Miss Jerrold, I gather?' Antony smiled as he spoke.

65

'Oh yes, of course I do, but then I'm different. I'm in love with him,' she said simply. 'And you needn't remind me it's hopeless Desmond, even if that woman does manage to divorce him. His principles wouldn't let him marry me, and I like him just as he is, I wouldn't want him to be different.'

'He has some good friends,' said Maitland, deliberately vague.

'And some not so good. Mr Stowe has already taken his affairs out of the firm's hands, and I'm sure when Mr Marrie gets round to it . . . but why did you want to see me? I don't know anything, only that he couldn't possibly have done the things she says he did.'

For the first time Antony was realising that his companion had led him into an embarrassing situation. 'Miss Jerrold,' he said and stopped. 'It isn't your evidence I want,' he went on.

'It can't be because I haven't any. I mean, I've never liked Elizabeth but naturally people would say that's just jealousy.'

'I'm afraid they would. And since you've done me the honour of being so frank with me, Miss Jerrold, perhaps you won't take it amiss if I offer you a word of warning. If the defence finds itself in any difficulties in the libel suit, they may try to drag your name into it.'

'I don't see how they could do that. There's never been anything between us. I don't even know if Edward likes me.'

'But you know him socially as well as a business associate?'

'Yes, the firm has always been a very friendly place and I've been there three years now, since a little while before he married.'

'Did you know Elizabeth Coke before that time?'

'No, I didn't. I attended the wedding, of course, and she was very sweet to me, rather condescending. I never said that to anyone else yet,' she added with a smile, 'because it sounds so catty. All the men were obviously bowled over by her, she's a very charming woman, and most of the women who were meeting her for the first time seemed to take her just at her face value. If I'd said it to you, Desmond, that's what you'd have thought, isn't it?'

'No, I shouldn't,' said Desmond stoutly. 'Anyway, I didn't know then –'

'Well, neither did I. It's only in the last year –' She hesitated and then went on firmly. 'Since I've been so frank with you I may as well say it all, Mr Maitland. It seemed a funny thing to think about a married man but I began to sense that he was very lonely. We did talk more, it always began with business matters, of course, and went on from there. After a while it made me examine my own feelings and that's when I realised how I felt about him. I suppose I'm not a very good actress,' she added sadly, 'and it was obvious to everybody, just as it seems to have been to Desmond.'

'You told me about it yourself,' Desmond reminded her.

'Yes, but only when I was sure you knew already.'

'That doesn't matter,' Maitland told her, 'it could only be conjecture at best, a matter of opinion, of no interest to the court. But could it be said, for instance, that you spent longer with him alone than these business matters you spoke of really required?'

'Well, we certainly spent longer together than we had done before, sometimes he'd suggest I go to his room for morning coffee or afternoon tea, and then we just talked about anything at all. People may have noticed, especially Miss Bagley, she's Edward's secretary, and was with his father when he was alive. I think she likes me and she's certainly fond of Edward so she wouldn't say anything more than was true. But if she was on oath she might feel she had to say she'd noticed the difference.'

'Yes, I can see that. And did these encounters in the office lead to anything more Miss Jerrold?'

'I told you there was nothing at all of that sort between us.'

He smiled at her suddenly. 'You forget I've met Mr Edward Coke,' he told her.

'You mean he has – integrity,' she said, hesitating over the word. 'That's perfectly true, but I do assure you again that I've no idea whether he cared for me at all. You were asking –'

'I only meant, were there any meetings outside the office that anyone could have known about?'

'We had dinner together twice when we were working late and Elizabeth was away.'

'That doesn't sound terribly abandoned. From our client's point of view I don't think we need worry too much about this aspect of things,' he added, turning to Desmond. 'At least, not as far as the libel action is concerned. After all, Mrs Coke is trying to convey the impression that her husband has no personal interest in sexual matters. She wouldn't want to spoil that picture of him.'

'You said, so far as the libel action is concerned,' said Desmond. 'Supposing we win?'

'In that unlikely event it might be a different matter when the divorce hearing came on.'

'What do you think Elizabeth would do?'

'I think she might very well abandon the petition for the time being, wait until the three years were up and try in the meantime to get some evidence of infidelity. I'm glad to have had the chance of talking with you, Miss Jerrold, because I think even these innocent meetings of yours must stop for the moment. Will you take my advice about that?'

'Yes, of course. I wouldn't do anything to hurt Edward, and even if I were a completely selfish person,' she added, 'it wouldn't do any good. Divorce or no divorce it wouldn't make any difference to him. And I think I'd have had sense enough to be careful anyway, Mr Maitland, because I'm quite sure that Elizabeth suspects something of how I feel.'

'Does she though? You said that when you met her first at the wedding she was cordial but condescending.'

'Yes, that's right. But lately when I've met her – sometimes she comes to the office, and sometimes Desmond and I have been asked to dinner at their house – I've seen her looking at me a little oddly, and some of her remarks seemed rather sarcastic. I don't know if you know what I mean.'

'To use your own word, catty,' said Antony, and wrenched the conversation rather abruptly on to a different course. 'As long as we're here, do you know David Barrie?'

'He's been present at some of those dinner parties I mentioned. I can't say I liked him very much. If *he* had some rather bizarre habits, as they say Edward has, it wouldn't surprise me a bit.'

'But you don't know anything to confirm that?'

'No, and I dare say I'm prejudiced because I hate what he and Elizabeth are doing so much.'

'I gather you also know Mr and Mrs Stowe.'

'Not well. I've met them at the Cokes in the same way as I did David Barrie. Were they talking about me?' she asked suspiciously.

'Your name was mentioned.' Antony was vague again. 'Drink up, Miss Jerrold, and we'll have another before we all go our separate ways.'

VIII

Maitland got home about seven o'clock to a house that was

69

quiet and might have been deserted, except for Gibbs, Sir Nicholas's cross-grained old butler who refused to retire, who was hovering in his usual place in the back of the hall. The study, which was Sir Nicholas's favourite room and the one he and Vera usually used, was in darkness. 'Lady Harding and Mrs Maitland came in some time ago,' Gibbs told him, contriving to make even this simple statement sound disapproving. 'You'll find them both upstairs.'

'Where's my uncle?'

'Sir Nicholas, as you may recall,' (as you ought to have remembered, said his tone) 'is dining with Mr Halloran.'

'Oh yes, of course. Thank you, Gibbs. Good night.' Vera he recalled as he went upstairs, as a former member of the bar had also been invited, but had made her excuses, feeling that she would be out of place in an otherwise completely male gathering. And, he suddenly remembered, Jenny had said something about teaching their aunt to drive. He went up the last flight of stairs two at a time in spite of his tiredness, and burst into the living room before his wife had time to come into the hall to greet him.

'You're both still alive?' he asked anxiously.

'Obviously,' said Vera, turning round to smile at him. She was sharing the sofa with Jenny, and her thick greying hair was escaping from the confining pins with even more abandon than usual. 'Been having my first driving lesson,' she said proudly. 'Or is that what you meant?'

'I'll get you a drink,' said Jenny, 'but I warn you we're one ahead.' She went to the table in the corner to pour sherry, probably thinking he needed something to soothe his fears. 'Vera is going to be a very good driver,' she said firmly, but her back was to the room and he couldn't see her expression.

'For that matter,' he said, going across to his usual place on the hearth rug, 'I'm two ahead of you but they were very

70

short measures. Shall I put a match to the fire, it's beginning to get chilly?'

'I think that's a very good idea,' said Jenny coming back towards him. 'Here's your sherry, Antony. Drink it and stop looking so suspicious.'

'Think he's every right to be,' said Vera. 'If you want to know the truth of it, I think I'm naturally ham-fisted,' she added, not being the purist her husband was in matters of the spoken word.

'As long as you don't kill the pair of you,' said Antony doubtfully. 'Central London is no place to make a start in.'

'We stayed in the park as much as we could,' said Jenny, 'and I don't agree with you, if you can drive in London you can drive anywhere.'

'Thinking of my time of life,' said Vera. 'No age to be making a start.' She paused, looking up at him keenly in a way that he found uncomfortably reminiscent of the manner his uncle sometimes adopted. 'Talking for the sake of talking,' she said. 'Something's bothering you.'

The fire was burning up nicely and even when he stood as he usually did, slightly to one side, the warmth was beginning to get uncomfortable. He took his glass from the mantel near the clock and went to sit in the chair that Sir Nicholas usually occupied. 'It's the case we were talking about the other night,' he said, 'when Uncle Nick remarked that Mallory must be developing a sense of humour, pitting the two of us against each other. It's a very nasty business.'

'Are you committed to accepting the brief?'

'Yes, I am.'

'And Nicholas told you, I suppose, that he's just accepted the defence in the libel suit.'

'Yes, he told me that. I'm rather glad he's out tonight, Vera, because I'd like to talk to you about it and I couldn't if he was here. And for the first time in his life,' he added with some satisfaction, 'he can't complain about my keeping him in the dark.'

'Safe with me,' said Vera.

'I know that. The thing is, I've been talking to all these people today –'

'What people?' said Vera, who liked to get things straight.

'Owen Barrie for one, the father of one of Uncle Nick's main witnesses. Also to a girl who is in love quite hopelessly with my client.'

'Poor girl,' said Jenny. 'Doesn't he return her affections?'

'You've forgotten what I told you about him. He doesn't believe in divorce and certainly wouldn't remarry even if his wife gets her way. So no happy ending there, I'm afraid.'

'Having listened for years to Uncle Nick's lectures on the sanctity of married life,' said Jenny, 'I suppose I ought to applaud that decision, but I can't help feeling sorry for her.'

'Well, so do I, because she's one of those loving and giving people, who quite genuinely puts his interests before hers. But as far as this case is concerned she's no earthly use to us, it was just that Desmond – that's my instructing solicitor, Vera – wanted me to warn her of the possibilities, in case the libel action goes our way.'

'You don't sound very hopeful.'

'I'm not. The other people I've seen are the witnesses to the publication of the libel and the damage done to my client's reputation. They're close friends of the family, and I must admit I hoped I'd get a lead somewhere.'

'What sort of a lead?'

'To disproving Mrs Coke's story.'

'Have to say it to you, Antony, Nicholas isn't easily taken in.'

'No, I'm quite aware of that. Bellerby is a different matter. Geoffrey and I have a joke that he's the supreme advocate of kindness to clients. All the same, you know, Uncle Nick could be wrong.'

'And so could you,' said Vera bluntly.

'I don't think I am, because I've come up with a theory that might explain Mrs Coke's actions. But Edward Coke has nothing to gain except the satisfaction of adhering to his principles.'

'And this other witness, the one who backs up her story?'

'He's more of a puzzle, but my theory goes some way to explaining his actions too. I think Elizabeth Coke was a gold digger, I think she took that job with Edward Coke's Aunt Harriet because she hoped to get a legacy out of it, if not some more immediate pecuniary advantage.' He went on to explain his ideas in much the same words as he had used to Desmond Barleycorn. 'That would account for everything, Vera,' he concluded. 'Don't you think?'

'Don't like the sound of it,' said Vera.

'But do you think there may be something in it?' he insisted.

'Afraid I do.'

'Vera, I'm sorry. I know you want Uncle Nick to be right.'

'Not to the extent of getting the wrong verdict,' said Vera. 'And from what you say you've nothing to go on but a lot of speculation, which could hardly be put forward in court. No evidence at all.'

'That's true, that's what's worrying me. I've no case and all I can do is go into court and do the best I can in cross-examination. You know what a hopeless job that can be. For myself I don't care a jot about winning or losing –'

'Don't you, Antony?' queried Vera, with what in her passed for gentleness.

He didn't pretend to misunderstand her. 'Well . . . perhaps. I admit most of my clients are out and out villains, but most of them have something likeable about them too. But if they're guilty at least I can comfort myself with that reflection, where with Edward Coke I'm absolutely certain . . . and it's such a beastly thing he's being accused of too.'

'In this particular case–' said Vera, the literal-minded.

'I know, I know, he's doing the accusing. But you know precisely what I mean, Vera.'

'So I do,' she concurred. 'Couldn't you persuade him to let the divorce go through undefended as soon as the three years are up? Even if it does he needn't compromise his principles at all.'

'I tried that at the beginning, but he wouldn't budge an inch. In any case the story's got about now to all their circle of friends. he's lost at least one client, and I shouldn't think it will be long before the rest of them hear about it too.'

'Yes, it's a pretty bad situation. Is there anything I can do, Antony?'

'Not a thing except help me steer the conversation away from the subject when we are all together,' said Antony ruefully. 'It's the first time I haven't been able to discuss a case with Uncle Nick, love,' he said later to Jenny when they were alone, 'and I can't say I like the situation one little bit.'

PART II

Coke versus Coke

Trinity Term, 1973

Wednesday, the first day of the trial

I

Sir Nicholas, however, seemed to bear with equanimity the state of affairs that troubled his nephew so much. The Easter recess came and went, new sets of papers came into chambers and were accepted or rejected according to old Mr Mallory's whim. In Maitland's room there were several anxious conferences with Desmond Barleycorn and Edward Coke in attendance, and Antony co-opted his friend and associate Derek Stringer, who was also in Sir Nicholas's chambers, to act as his junior when they got into court. Derek had an amused look when he knew Sir Nicholas would be defending, but Antony was by no means convinced that he took Edward Coke's protestations at face value. 'Too good to be true,' he said once, shaking his head sadly as the two solicitors left. But they had acted together many times before, and almost as often disagreed about their clients' guilt or innocence. Maitland had no doubt at all that Derek, whatever his feelings, would back him up to the hilt.

The last time he had appeared in a libel action Bruce Halloran had been prosecuting, and he himself, again with Stringer as his junior, had been defending. It was odd to have Sir Nicholas in opposition, with his junior, Mr Hawthorne, a young man of very little experience but quite capable of taking the note. It occurred to Maitland for the first time, looking at them – and later he considered himself to have been naive to be so slow in the uptake – that Mallory wouldn't have been so insistent in persuading his principal to take the brief if a good fee hadn't been involved. Not that

Sir Nicholas hadn't acted time and again for little or no remuneration, but he'd never done that with his clerk's consent. Someone must be footing the bill, Elizabeth Coke was unlikely to have much money of her own, he thought he saw Owen Barrie's hand in this.

But one thing wasn't changed from the last time he had appeared in a libel action, Mr Justice Lovejoy was on the bench. To Maitland's certain knowledge he had been talking for at least five years of retirement, but looking at him now – a tall man, impressive in his robes – he showed no sign that it was imminent or even desirable. It was said of him sometimes that he was slow of understanding, a fiction invented by those members of the bar who had appeared for him and been troubled by his habit of incessant questioning. Maitland's only thought that morning was that perhaps it might be better for the prosecution if the tale were true.

He was quite accustomed to maintaining a confident air in court, even when he was pretty sure in his own mind that his case was hopeless, but this morning, making his opening remarks, this proved to be more difficult than usual, perhaps because he was perfectly well aware that Sir Nicholas knew as well as he did that the prosecution weren't going to be able to prove their point. He had no doubt at all that Vera had kept her part of the bargain and refrained from discussing his side of the case with her husband, but Uncle Nick knew him so well, far too well for comfort. 'This is a particularly distressing case, my lord,' he began, 'not only because the matter alleged against my client is so unpleasant, but because it involves a matrimonial dispute, a falling out between two people who should be most closely united. I must apologise therefore before I begin that the facts I shall adduce are so distasteful, not only to your lordship, but also to the members of the jury, particularly to the ladies among them. It seems that . . .'

This was pure routine, he knew what he had to say by heart, and half of his mind at least was free to roam over other matters in an undisciplined way. He was thinking that the three women members of the jury were a particularly tough looking lot, and probably less likely than he was (though he considered himself to be past astonishment) to be shocked by what they heard. He was also remembering a little vaguely an earlier libel action of which he had read, where the judges had invited those ladies who were present among the spectators to withdraw, for fear their sensibility should be offended. Not one of them had done so. And in this day and age was it possible to elicit sympathy for a man falsely maligned, however unnatural the practices of which he was accused? He did his best with the facts however, though they occupied more time than he had intended to allot to them, so that he was reduced at last to watching Derek Stringer's right hand moving smoothly across his notepad. His junior, he knew, would give him a sign when he considered enough had been said. There it was now . . . Derek dropped his pen and rubbed his hand as if his fingers were growing tired. 'Mrs Coke's defence, my lord,' Maitland concluded hastily, 'according to the pleadings is one of justification. I hope we shall be able to demonstrate to you and to the members of the jury the sheer unlikelihood of this. I need not dwell upon the fact that the old saying, the greater the truth the greater the libel, is no longer true. I am sure that your lordship will be at pains to disabuse their minds of any such thoughts when your summing up is reached.'

'I am obliged by your confidence in me, Mr Maitland,' said Mr Justice Lovejoy dryly as counsel sat down again. 'Though I should have thought it was rather the defence's place . . . however.' He glanced at his watch. 'We were a

79

little late in starting, and as these remarks of yours have taken some time perhaps we had better adjourn for the luncheon recess without delay.'

'Not bad at all,' Sir Nicholas murmured as his nephew passed him on his way out of court, 'considering that we're both perfectly well aware that you have nothing whatever on which to base this optimism.'

Maitland grinned at him and essayed an enigmatic look. But it was no use; as he had thought as he started his speech, Sir Nicholas knew him far too well.

As soon as they reconvened after lunch Primrose Ross was called. She was inclined to twitter today, as Maitland rather unkindly called it in his own mind, but from the prosecution's point of view her account of receiving the letter – which was simultaneously introduced into evidence – was quite clear. It was obvious that she took her oath seriously. The rest of what she had to say in direct examination followed closely on her answers to his questions when he saw her before, but all the same Maitland felt a twinge of anxiety as Sir Nicholas rose to cross-examine. He had a feeling that, as a witness, Miss Ross might prove more of a liability than an asset.

'Now madam, my learned friend, Mr Maitland,' began Sir Nicholas (only too obviously just stopping himself from saying 'My nephew'), 'has very properly refrained from questioning you too closely on the contents of this letter. I don't wish to distress a lady of your sensibility, but there are one or two things I must ask you. For instance, I imagine I am not alone in finding it a little strange that you gave Mr Edward Coke this communication.'

'I couldn't contain myself!' said Primrose. 'You're quite right about this being a shock to me,' – this was a rather free interpretation of what Sir Nicholas had said but he made no attempt to contradict it – 'my friend Elizabeth, as you must know for yourself because you're acting for her, is such a dear person I couldn't bear to think of her being subjected to such treatment, not once, I gathered, but many times.'

'You had no hesitation then in accepting what she said?'

'No hesitation at all. She wouldn't tell a lie, and about such a matter –'

'Quite, quite. You told my – my learned friend that much the same sentiment had prompted Mrs Coke to write to you. That she couldn't contain her anger at what had happened.'

'That's quite true. She stood it as long as she could and then she left him, and as everything had to become public now I suppose she thought there was no harm in confiding in me. I think I may claim to be her closest friend.'

'My friend also suggested to you there was a certain rather gloating note in the letter.'

'That's what he said, but I don't agree at all. Of course she was pleased with the idea of being free from such a monster.'

'Thank you, Miss Ross,' Sir Nicholas, thought his nephew uncharitably, was almost purring. 'Have I got this right? Your first impulse was to see Mr Coke himself.'

'Oh no, not at all. The first thing I did was to ring Elizabeth. She had gone to an hotel, and written to me on their writing paper.'

'I see. And she confirmed what she had told you?'

'That wasn't why I called her at all, I wanted to know if she was all right. I'd have been very glad for her to stay with me if she wanted companionship, but she said she'd rather be alone.'

That, thought Maitland sadly, had been another dead end. Desmond Barleycorn had put his favourite firm of enquiry agents on to the case, but Mrs Coke's behaviour ever since she left her husband had been completely above reproach.

'Then you went to see Mr Coke?' Sir Nicholas was continuing.

'No ... no. I talked to two women friends first, Fran Walpole and Joanna Stowe. Only you know' – her manner became confidential and Antony almost began to suspect that she was enjoying herself – 'talking to them seemed to bring it home to me all the more. I was absolutely furious, and when Edward came to see me ... that's how it was, not the other way around.'

'Indeed?' said Sir Nicholas, exactly as though he hadn't known it all the time. For some reason – probably devious, thought Maitland rather crossly – he must have felt the statement would be more impressive coming from the witness herself.

'Yes, and he began denying everything, so I just thrust the letter into his hands and said 'See!' And he kept it!'

'Against your wishes?'

'Well ... not exactly. To tell you the truth I forgot to ask for it back.'

'Yes, I understand now, Miss Ross. Thank you. I think that is all I have to ask you.'

Maitland was on his feet again almost before his uncle sat down. 'Just two things, Miss Ross,' he said.

'Yes, what are they?'

'When you spoke to Mrs Coke, was anything said about your intention to confide her affairs to other people?'

'I thought it only right that their friends should know.'

'Yes, but that wasn't what I asked you. Was anything said when you spoke to Mrs Coke?'

'Not in so many words, but I think she knew what I intended. I said something like, 'It's so wicked, everyone should know,' and she didn't contradict me.'

'I see. And you found nothing surprising in her letter?'

'Shocking, yes. Surprising, no.'

'I have been thinking, Miss Ross –'

'Two questions you said, Mr Maitland,' the judge put in.

'I beg your lordship's pardon. It has just occurred to me .. may I have your lordship's permission to ask one more thing?'

Mr Justice Lovejoy inclined his head. He wasn't one of Maitland's sympathisers, considering his ways unorthodox and that he was as likely as not to inaugurate an unsuitable display of fireworks in court. 'If you wish, Mr Maitland,' he said, with only a little coldness in his voice. 'Perhaps it will clear the point I was just about to put to the witness myself.'

Maitland turned back to Primrose. 'Put yourself for a moment in your friend's place,' he said. 'In Elizabeth Coke's place. Considering the events she describes, don't you think you would have left your husband after the first such episode?'

'I should.' She smiled at him suddenly, and for the first time he realised that to some people she must appear quite an attractive woman. 'But Elizabeth is different you see, she's so good. I'm sure she thought something like, he'll get over it, or, perhaps I can persuade him to love me properly. Only then suddenly she realised that was never going to happen.'

'Thank you, Miss Ross, that is all.' If there was a faintly hollow note in Maitland's gratitude it wasn't to be wondered at. That was one question that had gone badly astray. Sir Nicholas threw a sardonic glance in his direction, Mr Justice Lovejoy was nodding as though that were indeed the question he had in mind. Miss Primrose Ross hesitated a moment and then stepped down from the witness box.

II

Frances Walpole was the next to take the stand and again

there were no surprises about what she had to say. It occurred to Maitland as he questioned her that there was something all wrong about talking to her like this, not in her husband's presence, because the two of them seemed to be truly a pair, as though one were not complete without the other. So they went through the story of Primrose Ross's visit, and Fran identified the letter she had been shown, and told him again of her talk that evening with her husband. And again Antony watched his uncle rise to cross-examine with a certain amount of trepidation. He hadn't been doing too well himself, considering that last disastrous question to Primrose Ross, but he had no expectation at all that Sir Nicholas would be guilty of a similar indiscretion.

'I can understand your reluctance, madam, in coming here today,' Sir Nicholas was beginning, when – regardless of courtroom etiquette – the witness interrupted him.

'Oh no, I wasn't reluctant at all.'

'You don't find the matter under discussion a trifle – shall we say, embarrassing?'

'I don't like it,' Frances admitted. 'On the other hand everyone knows there are men like that, it's nothing to be mealy-mouthed about. But what I meant was I wanted to tell everyone that Edward couldn't possibly be involved in a thing like that.'

'Perhaps, Mrs Walpole, you can tell us the reason for your opinion.'

'If you mean, can I prove it, of course I can't. It's an opinion based on my knowledge of his character,' she added with dignity.

'And that, I suppose, is profound.'

'You're making fun of me,' she told him without animosity.

'I wouldn't dream of it, madam,' said Sir Nicholas hurriedly before the judge could speak. 'I should be

interested to know, however, how long you have known
Mr Edward Coke.'

'Ever since I married my husband. Eight years,' she
implemented. 'Long enough to realise –'

'I wonder if you know, Mrs Walpole, the phrase that any
barrister dreads hearing more than another.'

She frowned a little over the question. 'I suppose you
mean being told that your client is guilty,' she said
hesitantly. And then, 'This is a funny case, isn't it, because
Edward is bringing the charge but it's really he who's
being accused?'

'Yes, but your reading of my meaning wasn't quite
correct. I meant the phrase used by so many prospective
witnesses about someone who happens to be a friend of
theirs.'

'I don't know, of course, how should I?'

'We hear it over and over again. They say, "He – or she of
course – wouldn't do a thing like that." But you know,
madam,' – Sir Nicholas was becoming avuncular, as that
word is commonly defined, though Maitland would have
argued the point any day – 'that the longer I live the more I
realise you can't say that about anyone. You just never
know.'

She smiled at him disarmingly. 'I dare say you're right,'
she said. 'I know I wouldn't presume to say of anyone, even
of Roland, that I knew him through and through. But there
are things ... and you know, if I can't say I'm sure about
Edward's essential goodness, how can you say it about
Elizabeth? Because that's what you're doing, isn't it? One of
them must be lying.'

There was no denying that Sir Nicholas looked a little
taken aback by this attack. He carefully avoided his
nephew's eye. His lordship seemed about to speak,
probably to utter some stinging rebuke. 'We mustn't fall
into an argument,' said Counsel, rather weakly. 'Could you

tell me, Mrs Walpole, did you speak of this matter to anyone else?'

'Only to Roland. I've just told you that. It seemed to both of us to be better not to mention it. Other people might believe it.'

'You mean, I think, that other people might not be so trusting as you. Miss Ross, for instance, took the letter at face value.'

'Well, yes, she did. But then she's completely blind to Elizabeth's faults.'

'As you are not?'

'Oh dear, I walked into that one, didn't I?' Her glance around the court appealed for sympathy but Antony was very much afraid the damage had been done. Sir Nicholas smiled at the witness affably, as well he might. 'I think, madam,' he said gently, 'we'd better leave matters there.' His learned friend, Mr Maitland, chose not to cross-examine.

Fran Walpole was rapidly succeeded in the witness box by her husband, who succeeded as he finished taking the oath in catching his wife's eye as she sat now in the body of the court. A long look passed between them, and Antony thought suddenly, she's warning him of something. But perhaps it's only to be careful on Edward Coke's behalf.

However that may have been there was nothing unexpected about either examination or cross-examination. In fact Sir Nicholas never managed to cross-examine because Mr Justice Lovejoy took over himself at that point, though without eliciting anything that was helpful to either side. It was not too long before Roland Walpole was allowed to step down, and went to seat himself near Fran. Antony saw him take her hand and squeeze it, while she spoke to him in an urgent undertone. He wondered idly what might be passing between them, but hadn't time to elaborate on the thought before Joanna Stowe was produced.

This time the examination took longer. There was not only the publication of the libel to prove, but the damage that had been done to Coke's reputation with the Stowes at least, and the names of the people to whom the story had been passed on. Mr Justice Lovejoy leaned forward.

'Do you intend to call *all* these people, Mr Maitland?'

'No, indeed, my lord. We shall hear from this lady's husband, Mr Terence Stowe, and then I think the question of special damages, which is not really under dispute, will be sufficiently proved.'

'I'm relieved to hear it,' said the judge leaning back again in his chair.

Joanna was a sulky witness, and the examination in chief took some time. At last Sir Nicholas rose and eyed her warily. 'You have said, Mrs Stowe, that you took the letter immediately at face value. Had you any special reason for doing so?'

'I didn't know, of course, that Edward was denying what was said, but even if he was there were two witnesses to its truth.'

'Both people on whose integrity you could rely?'

'What had they to gain?' she asked him.

'You mustn't question counsel,' the judge admonished her, but almost simultaneously Sir Nicholas replied.

'What indeed?' He turned a little and spoke rhetorically, addressing the court at large. 'We are agreed, I believe, that this case is one that must be decided on the evidence, not on some fancied knowledge of character,' he said, and sat down quickly before the judge could speak.

Maitland let it pass because he really had no choice in the matter, and a moment later was going into the same detail with Terence Stowe.

Here the fact that the surgeon had removed his affairs

from Edward Coke's hands since he had heard the contents of the letter was of course a material one, but when it came to the question of character he was today unexpectedly subdued. Neither Antony himself, nor Sir Nicholas when it came to his turn, retained him very long.

As soon as the witness had stepped down Mr Justice Lovejoy adjourned the court until the following morning.

III

Maitland walked back to chambers with his uncle, and as soon as they had both ascertained that there was nothing to detain them they took a cab home together. 'So that completes your case,' said Sir Nicholas reflectively.

'Except for my client. Edward Coke will be giving evidence tomorrow.'

'His word against his wife's, and hers backed up by an independent witness. If you're counting on any startling revelations when you come to cross-examine those two, my dear boy, I think you're in for a disappointment.' He paused, but his nephew had nothing to say to that and after a moment he went on. 'I'm sorry to be at odds with you over this matter, Antony. Quite frankly, in the ordinary way I should enjoy the opportunity of crossing swords with you, but I've got a nasty feeling this matter has come to mean a good deal to you. It's a fault you should fight against, allowing yourself to become emotionally involved.'

'If you stop caring you might as well be dead,' said Antony, quite unconscious that he had made the remark many times before, and that it was one his uncle was quite familiar with.

'Yes, I suppose you're right. But I've become accustomed

to relying on your judgement –' He broke off there looking affronted when Maitland burst out laughing.

'May I say, sir, that hasn't always been very evident,' he remarked. 'I wonder what you'll think when you've heard my client's story in the morning.' But even as he spoke the dismal conviction stole over him that Edward Coke was going to make a very bad witness indeed.

Thursday, the second day of the trial

I

And the next morning he found that his premonition for once had been correct. As a solicitor Edward Coke might have been expected to be less disturbed than most men at finding himself in a court of law. Indeed he seemed calm enough, too calm really. And though he denied Elizabeth's story vehemently, he came over as a hard nosed puritan whom anybody, his counsel thought, might have suspected of having been so repressed as to be bound to break out somewhere, sometime, in some disagreeable way. Under Maitland's prompting he spoke of the damage he had suffered, the loss of friends, the loss of clients.

'But this was not,' Antony prompted him, 'your reason for bringing this action.'

'In a way it was,' said Coke annoyingly.

'Perhaps you could explain to the court exactly what you mean by that, Mr Coke,' said Antony. Perhaps it would have been better from the beginning to give the witness his head. His answers weren't always calculated to put the best construction on things.

'Oh ... yes. I mean, I don't want people to think such things of me, and naturally I don't want my practice to suffer, but I'm not in it for the money. I don't want any damages from my wife.'

'I'm sure that the jury will find your attitude very under-standable,' said Maitland, hiding well enough his certainty that this was a lie. 'I think that's all I need to ask you for the moment, Mr Coke.' He sat down and watched – this time with extreme anxiety – as Sir Nicholas rose to his feet in his leisurely way.

'Mr Coke,' he said. 'You have heard the letter read in court that your wife wrote to her friend Miss Primrose Ross, I'm sure under the influence of great emotion. Are you telling us now that there is no truth in it?'

'I thought I'd made that clear. It's a lie from beginning to end.'

'I wonder if you are aware that Mr David Barrie is willing to give testimony in support of your wife.'

'So I've been told. But a fellow like that –'

'Like what, Mr Coke.'

'I don't think he has any moral sense at all,' said Edward defiantly.

'That is a very serious charge to make. However, the jury will make their own decision. But let us probe this matter a little further. My learned friend, Mr Maitland, has not called any witnesses in support of your denials. No facts, Mr Coke, only opinions.'

'That's very true, but it's next to impossible to prove a negative,' Edward replied, saying the right thing for almost the first time since he went into the witness box.

'It would have been helpful, however,' said Sir Nicholas thoughtfully, 'if some support for your story could have been found. Can you think of any reason why Mrs Coke should be lying?'

'Because she wants a divorce right away, and the way the law stands at present –'

'Ah yes. But that argues a singular impatience, if there is no deeper reason for it. I suggest to you, Mr Coke, that the reason is quite a simple one: that her life with you had become completely insupportable.'

'I offered her a separation, and an allowance.'

'You yourself consider the marriage bond a very sacred one.'

'I do indeed.'

'Then will you not give Mrs Coke credit for perhaps having similar feelings?'

'She doesn't care about it at all. I thought she did at first but now I've discovered I was wrong.'

'She may not consider it in quite the same light that you do, but a mere separation might not be sufficient reassurance to a terrified woman. A complete break would be the only thing that could satisfy her.'

'I never laid a finger on Elizabeth in my life.'

'That's an unfortunate way of putting it, Mr Coke, because that is one of her complaints against you. That your marriage was never consummated.'

'That's another lie. We lived together as man and wife in the ordinary way for three or four months after the marriage. Then she declined to continue the relationship on those lines, and finally elected to have her own bedroom.'

'To which you consented?'

'I had no choice.'

'In any case Mr Coke, you will agree with me I think that there are other ways of intimidation than physical ones. You have no living-in servants I believe.'

'Just a daily. She's always gone before I get home from the office.'

'Do you deny that during the last six months or so David Barrie has been a frequent visitor to your house?'

'No, I don't deny it. It's true.'

'Just during the last six months?' Sir Nicholas insisted.

'Before that he would come by invitation, generally with his father, and also generally we would ask other friends to meet them. I was surprised the first evening he turned up alone unexpectedly.'

'Unexpectedly, Mr Coke?'

'Unexpected by me. Elizabeth told me afterwards that

she thought he was lonely and that was half the trouble.'

The judge leaned forward. 'I think you're going to have to explain that remark, Mr Coke,' he said.

'Yes my lord. Elizabeth said his father was worried about him, Owen Barric that is. About David's way of life. She said –'

'Yes, that is quite enough, Mr Coke. Mr Maitland, perhaps you should have instructed your witness more fully on the occasions when hearsay evidence is or is not permissible,' said Lovejoy unfairly.

'I must apologise to your lordship,' said Antony, nobly repressing a desire to say, it was your question that set him off, and wondering at the same time whether some, at least, of the jury would be imaginative enough to fill in the blanks of Edward's explanation. 'Perhaps I may answer your lordship's question by saying that, as a result of what his wife told him, my client felt that her desire to entertain Mr David Barrie in their house frequently was not unreasonable.'

'I suppose we must be contented with that,' said the judge, with a glance at the witness that demonstrated anything but contentment. 'Sir Nicholas?'

'I must thank you, m'lud, for clarifying this matter for us,' said Sir Nicholas, allowing himself the touch of sarcasm that his nephew had forgone. He turned back to Edward Coke again.

'So David Barrie became a regular visitor. How regular?'

'I suppose he would dine with us once or twice a week.'

'Did it distress you at all to have what might have been tête-à-tête dinners with your wife interrupted in this way?'

'No, our estrangement had progressed too far for that. In a way it was more comfortable to have a third party present.'

'So you cannot deny, Mr Coke, that the opportunity for these episodes that Mrs Coke mentions existed.'

'No, but I can deny that anything like that ever happened.'

'Why did you oppose the divorce, Mr Coke?'

'I explained that to my own counsel. It was a matter of principle.'

'A rather stern principle, since it has got you into this predicament.'

'May I remind you, Sir Nicholas, that I am the plaintiff in this case?'

'I'm well aware of it. But the fact remains that the only reason for Mrs Coke bringing a divorce action on the grounds of exceptional depravity and exceptional hardship must be that the feeling of any bond at all between you had become completely intolerable.'

Maitland was on his feet. 'My lord,' he said.

'Yes, Mr Maitland?'

'My learned friend has referred on several occasions to the divorce action which is pending, but it is no part of these proceedings. The matter cited in the petition is privileged, this action is being brought on the grounds of the publication of a libel by means of a letter addressed to a friend of the defendant.'

'I think you have a point there, Mr Maitland,' said Mr Justice Lovejoy rather grudgingly. 'However, I admit myself to being a little puzzled by your client's attitude. All this very unpleasant business could have been avoided by his agreement in the matter of the divorce.'

'Could it, my lord? I'm in some doubt about that. I think that for some reason Mrs Coke wants her freedom now, this minute.'

'Mr Maitland! This is no time for a speech to the jury. And I think I should warn you now that if you attempt to address them on such lines I shall take the gravest exception.'

'If your lordship pleases.' Maitland sat down, not

altogether concealing a faintly mutinous feeling, but the interruption had had the intended effect.

'I think, Sir Nicholas,' said the judge, 'that enough has been said about people's motives, a matter which must be one for conjecture. Let us confine ourselves to the facts of the letter Mr Maitland mentioned.'

'Certainly, m'lud. That leaves me with only one question to ask,' said Sir Nicholas, but he didn't sound too distressed about that. He must know, thought Antony resentfully, that he has the whole thing in the bag already. 'You have read this letter, Mr Coke, the letter that was written by your wife to her friend Miss Primrose Ross. In this connection the word "gloating" has been used. Would you agree with that?'

Edward Coke frowned over the question for a moment, then his face cleared. 'It's one of those cases where I'm damned if I do and I'm damned if I don't,' he said almost cheerfully. Perhaps the mention of one final question made its own contribution to his change of mood.

'Really, Mr Maitland,' said Mr Justice Lovejoy, 'I must tell you for the second time that you really must keep your witness in better order.'

'I apologise to your lordship,' said Maitland gravely. But Edward Coke was already continuing.

'So I may as well tell the truth,' he said. 'I'm afraid it's obvious she did want the divorce immediately very badly, and her letter made it quite clear that she thought she was sure of getting it. I don't think gloating is too strong a word.'

'Thank you, Mr Coke, that's all I have to ask you. Unless my learned friend —'

Maitland shook his head. Quite enough damage had been done, he thought and he was impatient to hear what Elizabeth Coke had to say.

But before that, of course, there was Sir Nicholas's opening address, which occupied the court until lunchtime. Not over-long, because Edward Coke's testimony had taken up a considerable slice of the morning session, but damnably effective for all that. Which was only to be expected, his uncle was an old campaigner, and not at all likely to miss any opportunity that offered, particularly when he believed whole-heartedly in his client's wrongs. Antony listened without any enjoyment at all, and was hard put to it to maintain an equable mood at the luncheon table. But the curiosity persisted and he went back to court quite eagerly.

Elizabeth Coke was a slender woman with a fragile air about her, conservatively dressed, though Antony suspected that Jenny might have had a word or two to say about the perfection of the cut of her dark grey suit. Her hair was fair and probably naturally curly, and if he thought she had overdone the pallor a bit by an over-use of face powder nothing could have been more effective. Unless it was the gentle respectfulness of her manner towards the court. In watching her he had to admit that if this was acting it was first-class of its kind.

Clearly the story that she had to tell distressed her. Sir Nicholas took her through her married life from the beginning, in fact he went back a little to stress what Antony had disrespectfully called the ministering-angel role, as it applied to Edward's Aunt Harriet. 'He's a good looking man,' she said, carefully not looking across the court to where her husband was now seated, 'and perhaps I was too ready to believe myself in love. In any case we were married within a very few months and it was only then that I discovered my mistake.'

'I'm sorry to distress you with these details, Mrs Coke,

but the court must know what you mean by that.'

'That I'd expected a normal married life, the sort of thing every girl dreams of,' said Elizabeth earnestly. 'Instead of that . . . we shared a room at first but never 'slept together' in the way most people mean when they use that phrase, and after a while he suggested that I should move into the spare room and by then I was only too glad to do so. I don't think our friends suspected anything wrong at that stage, but of course the feeling of closeness we'd had – or I'd thought we'd had – was gone for good. And as time went on the feeling of strangeness, I think I mean of being strangers to each other, just seemed to increase.'

'And there is something else I must ask you, Mrs Coke. Were you a virgin when you married?'

'Yes, I was.'

'Was the question of your marital relations ever raised between you and your husband?'

'Of course it was. Not at first, of course. I thought this was something new for both of us, it would take time to settle down. But I wanted children, I told him that.'

'And what did he say?'

'Nothing at all. He just looked at me for a long time and then walked out of the room and closed the door. After that I didn't feel that I ever could bring up the subject again.'

'How long did this state of affairs persist?'

'About two years as near as I could say. I ought to tell you, perhaps, that Edward used to disappear sometimes in the evening and not come home until very late. I thought then that perhaps he found other women more attractive than I, but now I think –'

Maitland was on his feet. Sir Nicholas interrupted suavely. 'We're getting into the realms of conjecture again, Mrs Coke, and unless you have any proof to offer I'm sure his lordship will not permit this sort of speculation.'

'Oh, I'm sorry. I thought you wanted to know everything.'

'Everything that you know, of your own knowledge. And everything that you can prove by bringing a witness that your word is true. I realise that this must be very distressing for you,' said Sir Nicholas again, unnecessarily as his nephew considered.

'Oh, it is!'

'You were telling us that during the first two years of your marriage your relationship with your husband deteriorated gradually. Did you consider leaving him?'

'I thought about it, of course. But I'd taken a vow, you know, for better or worse, and I kept hoping . . . I suppose it was silly of me, but I thought he'd loved me in the beginning and perhaps he would again.'

'Did you consult a solicitor?'

'Oh no!'

'What happened at the end of the two years, six months ago in fact, that changed matters?'

'Edward seemed to become more friendly with David Barrie. The Barries were friends of his and used to visit us quite often, in fact I think Mr Barrie – David's father – had been a friend of Edward's father. But then all of a sudden David started coming to dinner on his own, sometimes as often as twice a week. The first two or three times it happened I was surprised, and the more so because after dinner Edward would take the opportunity of leaving us alone together, and then coming into the room suddenly as though he expected something might be going on.'

'Had you given him any reason for these suspicions, Mrs Coke?'

'No reason in the world. I like both the Barries, and I think people are sometimes unjust to David, there's a lot more in him than appears on the surface. I mean, he's a far deeper, more sincere person. But I don't love him, I never have.'

Mr Justice Lovejoy leaned forward again. 'I hope Mr

Maitland will not object if I ask you what you thought this behaviour meant,' he said.

'It didn't occur to me immediately, my lord, but I think now that he hoped that there would be some attraction between us, and that he would be able to witness . . . need I go on?'

'I think the court will take your meaning, Mrs Coke. You are trying to tell us that your husband's sexual preferences are such that he prefers to be an onlooker rather than an active participant.'

'Yes, my lord, that's true.'

'You didn't realise at first, but later –' prompted Sir Nicholas.

'Later he insisted that we . . . that we make love to each other,' she said. 'I shouldn't talk about love in that context, it was nothing like that, but I don't know how else to put it and keep any dignity at all.'

She was nearly in tears by this time and Sir Nicholas hastened to reassure her. 'I think his lordship has explained the position very well, and the jury will under-stand your reluctance,' he said. 'There is, however, one question which I am sure my learned friend will ask you when he comes to cross-examine. Why did you agree to this – this play-acting?'

'Partly because I was afraid not to.'

'Your husband has abused you physically perhaps?'

'No, he never struck me. The most wounding thing, I suppose, was his sarcasm, I don't know if you, being a man, can understand how that would affect me. Also he treated me as a possession, someone completely subject to his will. And then, in face of what was obviously a perversion – something I never dreamed could happen to me – I didn't know how far he might go if he were thwarted. I thought it might have provoked a quite mad kind of anger, there was certainly a wild look in his eye that was quite unlike anything I had ever seen in him before, and as I say I thought if we didn't do as he asked there might be quite disastrous results for all of us.'

'You thought in fact that he might go berserk with rage?'

'I thought he might murder David or me or both of us,' she said. Antony could have sworn she spoke reluctantly, and for the first time since he had formed his own conclusions about the matter an element of doubt crept into his mind. Which was the last thing he wanted at the moment.

'I see. And when the suggestion was first made, on the fourth visit as far as you remember, what was David Barrie's reaction? I don't want you to tell us, Mrs Coke,' he added hurriedly, 'what he thought about the matter, that will all come better from himself. But what you observed from his reaction, and what he said.'

'Well I think,' said Elizabeth, ignoring counsel's advice, 'that he felt much as I did. He stood looking at Edward as if he couldn't believe his ears, and then he looked at me and back at Edward again. And at last he came across to me, we were in the drawing room, you know, and I was standing near the sofa. And he put his hands on my shoulders and said quite quietly, "We'd better humour him." And then he said, "Don't worry, darling, I love you and I won't do anything to hurt you," and I couldn't find the words to tell him that I didn't love him at all.'

'And after that –'

'It was the first of many nights when we made love in Edward's presence. Afterwards he would seem calmer, pleasant with both of us, the good companion I had thought him to be in the early days before we were married. But I knew, of course, that what we were doing was wrong, we couldn't go on with it indefinitely, only it seemed such a dreadful thing to tell anybody about. But at last I did pluck up my courage and I went to see Mr Bellerby.'

'Mr Bellerby, my lord, is my instructing solicitor,' Sir

Nicholas explained before the obvious question could be asked that was hovering on the judge's lips. 'Did you tell David Barrie of your intention, Mrs Coke?'

'I didn't have a chance to say anything much to him, only once I whispered in his ear, "I'm going to put a stop to it." And I didn't talk to him about giving evidence, of course, Mr Bellerby did that, and he told me that David backed up my story absolutely. That was when I knew it was all right and I simply had to tell someone so I wrote to Primrose.'

'Believing that your letter would be seen by her eyes alone,' Sir Nicholas suggested. Maitland gave his uncle a rather sardonic look but said nothing.

'Yes, of course that's what I thought. I didn't dream that she'd show it to anybody else. And, of course, I didn't think there could be any harm in writing what was true.'

'You were quite right about that, Mrs Coke,' Sir Nicholas assured her. 'I've no more questions for you myself but I must ask you to stay where you are until we see whether your husband's counsel has anything to say to you. You needn't worry, we all realise the difficulty of your position, and I'm sure he'll be as gentle with you as I have tried to be.'

As far as Maitland was concerned that was true only because it would be good policy not to treat her roughly. After a number of years even the least sensitive of barristers gets a feeling for atmosphere; Maitland, unfortunately for himself, was perhaps more sensitive than most, and he was in no doubt at all that the feeling in the court that afternoon was strongly in the defendant's favour. All the same he couldn't let what she had said go altogether unchallenged. It was a delicate balance, and he hoped he could achieve it. 'My learned friend is right,' he said, 'It's a dreadful story indeed for a lady to have to tell in open court. I can only wonder why you laid yourself open to this embarrassment.'

'But I wrote the letter in all innocence, I didn't realise –'

'Forgive me, Mrs Coke, that wasn't what I meant.'

'But I have to tell it, Mr Bellerby said I must tell it. He said you could establish the libel quite easily, though I don't think it at all fair that a private letter should be made public like this. And he said that the only possible defence was – was justification.'

'Mr Bellerby was quite right,' said Maitland cordially. 'And you needn't remind me that you are here today because my client, your husband, has brought suit against you. I was referring to the fact that you were apparently willing to tell this tale in the course of the divorce proceedings.'

'Well, I had to. Mr Bellerby explained all that to me too. That you can't petition for divorce except in exceptional circumstances until you've been married for three years.'

'Six more months is not a very long time to wait.'

'But it would have been no different. Edward would never have agreed.'

'I think, however, that you could have satisfied the court of the irretrievable breakdown of your marriage without going into quite so much distressing detail.'

'Perhaps, but six months was too long. I couldn't go on as I was, it was so very wrong.'

'My client has told us that he offered you a separation.'

'Yes, he did, but I didn't think that was good enough. I know his views on marriage, you see, and I know it seems ridiculous to be so strict about one set of rules and so lax about another, but that's the way he is. I didn't think he'd ever let me go while I was still legally married to him. I thought that somehow the same thing might happen all over again.'

This time it was Sir Nicholas's eye that held a sardonic look, and his nephew couldn't wonder at it. 'I will follow your counsel's advice so far, Mrs Coke, as to say that I think we need not go any further into the details of this unpleasant allegation which my client has categorically denied. However, I hope you will not think me unreasonable if I tell you that there are one or two points I should like to have clarified. For instance, you describe David Barrie as a deeper, a more sensitive person than is generally supposed. In view of the part he took in these proceedings can you explain that remark?'

'But he is! I'm not condoning what he did any more than I'm condoning my own actions,' she said bravely, 'but he was very gentle with me, and heaven knows what would have happened if he hadn't agreed to do what Edward wanted.'

'That brings me to another point. You implied that you were fearful that your husband would injure you in a mad rage if you opposed him, in spite of the fact that you admit he never laid hands on you in anger.'

'I hoped I had made it clear that this was something about which he wasn't at all rational.'

'I see. You say it's a great sorrow to you, Mrs Coke, that your marriage was never consummated . . . a fact which, may I remind you, my client also denies?'

'I told you I wanted children.' And it was at this point, oddly enough, that Maitland became firmly convinced that she was lying and hardened his heart against her.

'Now let's return to the question of divorce,' he said. 'You became a Roman Catholic, did you not, before you married my client?'

'Edward says that in this context Roman is a contradiction in terms,' said Elizabeth, for the first time wandering from the point. 'But yes, that's true, I was received into the church.'

'And yet you feel there is nothing wrong in petitioning for divorce?'

'In certain circumstances –'

'As the marriage had not been consummated, according to your story, you could have asked for an annulment.'

'But Edward would never have agreed, and how could I have proved –'

'At least you could have asked for a dispensation on the grounds of exceptional hardship.'

'No, I didn't bother. I don't go to church now. If you want the whole story, I didn't really believe at all, only Edward wanted it and I didn't really care either way.'

'I'm surprised you found anyone to receive you then.'

'Oh, I didn't say that to anyone else. Edward would have had a fit, and I suppose I was silly enough to think that what was so near to his heart must be right. I was foolish, I think, but very much in love.'

Worse and worse, thought Maitland to himself. 'But you knew, I think, in fact you have already agreed, that your husband would oppose the matter, that even if you waited for six months and applied on the lesser grounds of the irretrievable breakdown of your marriage there would be some delay in the granting of a decree.'

'Yes, of course I knew that. Edward never made any secret of his prejudices.'

'Then may I suggest to you, Mrs Coke, with the greatest respect, that you had some reason for wanting a divorce quickly. I gather you yourself have no objection to remarriage.' He paused expectantly and after a moment she said:

'No, no objection at all.'

'Then I put it to you that your reason for wanting this divorce was because you wish to marry again; and your reason for wanting it quickly was because you were afraid, perhaps, that the man you intend to marry might change his mind.'

'That isn't so at all. Such an idea never entered my head.'

'Then before I sit down, Mrs Coke, may I leave you with

two ideas, on which I may say I shall elaborate when I come to address the jury? You were acting as nurse-companion to Edward Coke's aunt, Mrs Harriet Coke, when you first met him. She was a wealthy old lady, I think he had some expectation in that quarter which was disappointed when she died six months ago. It is almost exactly six months since these visits of David Barrie to your home began. Am I being too fanciful in imagining that there might be some connection?'

She went as white as a sheet at that, but though she made no reply there was defiance and naked hatred in the look she gave him. 'That is all, Mrs Coke,' he said gently.

As he sat down he felt the judge's eye upon him and wondered whether he was going to be asked to explain those remarks too. But evidently Mr Justice Lovejoy thought better of the idea. He settled back in his chair, watched Elizabeth Coke leave the stand with an indulgent eye, and seemed to be taking an interest in the young man who replaced her.

Maitland was taking his own interest in the witness and wondering as he did so whether his tactics were going to be justified. It had been open to him to be far more direct with Elizabeth Coke about her desire to marry, open to him too to call Owen Barrie for the purpose of establishing this. Rightly or wrongly he had felt that wasn't the right way to go about it, but now that it came to the point he was wondering, as was his way, whether that decision had been the right one.

His first thought as he looked at David Barrie was that he was a rather precious young man, though not effeminate in any way. In fact, he could see him very well as Bunthorne with a train of twenty lovesick maidens hanging on his every word. He was not very tall, and slender, and had a wave in his hair that was quite obviously encouraged, but though he had allowed it to grow rather long it was neat enough. In fact, 'neat' was a very good overall description of him, if you discounted the fact that he obviously patronised a very expensive tailor. Sir Nicholas was asking his preliminary questions with elaborate courtesy, so that Maitland, in spite of the seriousness of the situation, couldn't resist smiling to himself. In his uncle's eyes, as he knew well enough, Elizabeth Coke was an innocent victim; David Barrie as a witness to her wrongs must be treated with consideration, but that didn't make counsel like him or his ways any the better.

Sir Nicholas pursed his lips when he got the airy answer, 'Independent means,' to a question as to the witness's occupation, but he did not pursue the subject. Instead he asked, 'You are acquainted, I believe, with both the plaintiff and the defendant in this rather distressing case.'

'Yes, I've known Edward as long as I remember, and Elizabeth since the wedding, which I attended. Edward's father and mine were friends.'

'Will you tell us, Mr Barrie, in your own words how your relationship with the Cokes progressed after their marriage?'

'That's what I'm here for, isn't it?' said David cheerfully. 'When Edward was a bachelor, he used to dine with us sometimes and I might or might not be there, and every few months he'd give a party at a restaurant somewhere. After his marriage to Elizabeth he set about a course of rather formal entertaining, I was always asked at the same time as my father, with perhaps Primrose Ross and that girl Jerrold from Edward's office to make up numbers, and probably another married couple of their acquaintance as well. Rather a bore really, I only went along to oblige Dad. But after a while –'

'Yes, Mr Barrie?'

'Well, you've seen Elizabeth,' said David. He took a moment to look·round the court, inviting their sympathy.

'She's a stunning girl, wouldn't you say? I began to be very fond of her, only of course there was Edward and I knew enough about him to realise he'd never give her a divorce whatever happened.'

'But after a while you began to visit the Cokes more often. Can you tell me how that came about?'

'It was to oblige Edward.'

'You mean he was quite plain with you –'

'No, I don't mean that at all,' interrupted the witness hurriedly. 'He began by telling me how much he loved Elizabeth, what a good wife she was, things like that. And then he said that in spite of that they had very diverse interests, plays and art and ballet. Books, too. He said he was quite willing to conduct her to an occasional theatrical performance – that's how he put it – but he found himself unable to discuss these things with her intelligently, and he felt she was missing something, that was lacking in him. So if I would come round and see them fairly regularly he thought that would be a kindness she would appreciate.'

'And so you agreed.'

'I jumped at it,' said David frankly. 'Well, naturally. And I wasn't surprised, the first few times I went there, that he used to leave us alone together, because I thought it was in order that we should get on to these topics. But of course it wasn't easy for me because the more I fell for her.'

'And after these first few visits you mentioned?'

'That was when Edward suggested that we should embark on a more intimate relationship,' David replied. Antony thought he could hear Bellerby's voice there, prompting him, left to himself the young man would probably have been a good deal more forthright. 'It was pretty startling I can tell you. I was completely – well completely taken aback for a moment.'

'And then, Mr Barrie?'

'I think I protested a bit and Edward became more

insistent. He said there were precedents, and he said he wouldn't deny Elizabeth the pleasures of the flesh. I'm quoting him again. Quite frankly I thought him capable of anything in the way of violence at that moment and I went across to Elizabeth where she was standing by the couch. She had gone quite stiff with fright and I said something to her, trying to make her feel better. I can't remember what. And you know, sir, the suggestion was so much in accordance with my own wishes, only not there and then of course. And I wouldn't have forced her, but I could see that she was afraid of what Edward might do. And I was afraid for her. And so it happened.'

'And you went back to the house again, Mr Barrie, knowing that this scene would be repeated?' asked the judge suddenly.

'Well, yes, my lord. But before that I tried to get Elizabeth to leave him, it seemed like the only thing to do.'

'She wasn't willing to do so?'

'No, my lord. She said they'd only been married for two years and perhaps Edward might come round now to a more rational way of thinking. And when I pressed her she burst into tears and said, "I think if I left him he'd murder us both." And it seemed to me that, in the circumstances, if I didn't do what he wanted he'd get somebody else who might hurt her badly. I loved her at least, even if she didn't love me.'

'But eventually, in spite of this fear, she did decide to leave her husband?' said Sir Nicholas, when Mr Justice Lovejoy sat back, apparently satisfied.

'Yes, but I didn't know anything about that until the solicitor, Mr Bellerby, got in touch with me. I admit he had a bit of a time getting the story out of me, it wasn't one I was anxious to tell. But when I realised it was for Elizabeth's own good, of course I came out with the whole thing.'

'Thank you, Mr Barrie. I think before I let you go I must ask you to read the letter upon which this action is based.' There was a pause while the document in question was handed to the witness and he complied with Sir Nicholas's request. 'I must ask you to think very seriously,' said counsel at last. 'Are the facts stated in that letter exactly true, so far as they come within your knowledge, or do they deviate in any way from what happened?'

'They're true down to the last detail,' said David firmly. And turned a little as Sir Nicholas sat down, when he saw that Maitland was already on his feet.

'That's a very specious story, Mr Barrie,' said Antony amiably. 'Everything accounted for. Every action on your part and Mrs Coke's completely and rationally explained.'

'It was all true,' said David defiantly.

'Was it also true that you have no occupation?'

'A phrase that may cover a multitude of sins. No, my lord,' – as Mr Justice Lovejoy seemed about to speak – 'that was meant metaphorically, not literally. I just wished to find out from the witness whether he has not considerable time at his disposal during the day, when most people are busy at their offices.'

'You may answer counsel's question,' said the judge rather grumpily.

'I don't find the time hanging heavily upon me,' said David, smiling a little. 'But, no, I don't keep office hours of any kind.'

'Then even while she was living with her husband you had ample opportunity of talking to Mrs Elizabeth Coke during the day, and seeing her too if you wished.'

'I don't quite know what you're implying, but we didn't see each other in that way. I'd have been glad to, I'm honest enough to admit that, but Elizabeth would never agree.'

'And since she left the protection of her husband's house such meetings would have been even more easily arranged,' said Maitland, apparently ignoring the last answer.

'They could have been but they weren't.'

'Not even one meeting to arrange the details of this story you're telling us?'

'There was no need to confer together. We'd only to tell the truth.'

'Indeed? How affecting! Tell me one more thing, Mr Barrie,' – the words came out like the crack of a whip when the witness's mind was obviously firmly fixed elsewhere – 'did you know that Mrs Elizabeth Coke had agreed to marry your father as soon as her divorce was final?'

'That's not true!'

'I take it that the answer to my question is no.'

'It isn't true,' said the witness again doggedly. All trace of his debonair manner had left him.

'You may ask him for yourself tonight. Better still, you can ask Mrs Coke; but not, of course, until his lordship adjourns the hearing for the day.'

'I don't have to ask anybody.' But his eyes went across to Elizabeth and there was a beseeching look in them. 'I know it isn't true,' he said, with only the faintest hesitation in his voice, 'because she's going to marry me.'

III

'That was a nice little rabbit you pulled out of your hat,' said Sir Nicholas approvingly. He had been completely silent on the way home, so that Antony was wondering a little uneasily what exactly his sentiments were, but as soon as they were in the house his uncle said peremptorily, 'Come into the study,' and when they found themselves alone there produced his comment. 'But are you quite sure

110

it wouldn't have been more effective if you'd played it straight?'

'You must be deeply moved, Uncle Nick,' said Antony, taking a chair and watching his uncle pour sherry. 'I've never heard you mix your metaphors before, or come so near to the colloquialisms you abhor so much either.'

'Your aunt must be corrupting me,' said Sir Nicholas seriously. It was a matter of minor grievance with Antony that slang expressions would be tolerated from Vera that would have brought down the heavens on his own head. 'Where is she, by the way?' asked Sir Nicholas, looking round as though he might find his wife hiding in a corner of the room. 'Upstairs with Jenny?'

'Jenny said something about another driving lesson.'

'Heaven forbid!' said his uncle, blanching.

'I wish it would too, because I don't suppose it's the slightest use either of us saying anything,' said Antony, accepting a glass. 'But at least it's kept her out of court, and for some reason I wasn't too keen on her watching you wipe the floor with me.' But then his curiosity got the better of him. 'What do you think I should have done differently?'

'You could have called Owen Barrie to give evidence. I take it it was from him that you got your information.'

'It was. Ought we to be talking like this?' Maitland wondered.

'Why not? There's no further evidence to be called, no further cross-examination by either of us that might be influenced by the other's opinion.'

'Only our closing addresses.'

'Which are already written. At least, I hope you've not been so neglectful –'

'No, it's done, though I imagine yours will have to be slightly revised.' Sir Nicholas glanced at him sharply but for once in his life saw no signs that his nephew was being deliberately annoying. 'All right, Uncle Nick,' Antony went on. 'The way I work it out is this. If I'd called Owen Barrie I'd have demonstrated that Elizabeth had a motive for wanting a divorce; this way I achieved the same effect, and cast doubt on the story of one of your principal witnesses too. Without hurting a rather decent chap any more than I had to.'

'You mean Owen Barrie?'

'Yes, of course. I never talked to you about my meeting with him, but we got on famously on the whole. He'll be hurt when he hears of David's outburst, but not so much as if I'd hauled him into court himself.'

'That's all very well, but are you under the impression that you've completely discredited my client? Because –'

'I know, you spiked my guns neatly when you called her back to the stand. I wonder,' he added rather enviously, 'that you had the nerve.'

'Yes, I know what you're thinking. One should never ask a question in court unless one is quite certain of the answer. In this case I thought I was certain, Antony, and I got just what I wanted.'

'Yes, a very pretty little story,' Maitland conceded. 'She told the truth when she said she wasn't in love with David Barrie, but at least he was kind and quite normal, and after what had happened she felt it was her duty to marry him. I don't quite see that myself, but it sounded convincing enough. And, of course, Owen Barrie was just a friend, she couldn't think where I'd got the idea –'

'I notice you didn't cross-examine her again yourself.'

'I know when I've met my match. But to get back to her reasons for proposing to marry David Barrie –'

'In the matter of moral principles one might divide the modern world into three parts,' said Sir Nicholas (exactly as if he knows what he's talking about, thought Antony irreverently). 'There are those who areå.å.å. is chaste too

112

old fashioned a word for you to stomach?'

'It will pass.'

'Then there are those who are completely promiscuous,' said Sir Nicholas, well away on his exposition now. 'And the third class lies somewhere between the two, those who think there is no moral objection to indulging in sexual activity if marriage is their eventual goal. Mrs Coke, in spite of having acted under her husband's coercion, feels she has been doing something wrong and wants now to put it right.'

'Yes, I agree, she got over that impression very well. I'm sure the jury were impressed. What do you think will happen tomorrow?'

'I think they'll bring in a verdict in favour of my client, and to look a little further forward I think that when the divorce action is heard her petition will be granted.'

'After which we could launch a private action for perjury.'

'Which you would undoubtedly win. Against Elizabeth Coke and against David Barrie. But what good would it do your client?'

'No good in the world and I wasn't speaking seriously. One thing I will grant you, Uncle Nick, Elizabeth Coke is extremely impressive. I'm not a bit surprised she took you in.'

'Took me in?' said Sir Nicholas, outraged. 'I was never more sure of the truth of anything in my life.'

'Even after she was caught out in at least one lie under oath?'

'You knew my views on that subject,' his uncle told him, as indeed Antony did. They were very strict indeed. 'But it isn't everyone who shares them, and it's hardly fair to judge other people by one's own principles.'

'All right, you win.'

'I'm only surprised that once you had seen her, and heard

her story from her own lips, you didn't change your mind.'

'I did for a moment,' Maitland admitted. 'Well . . . almost.'

'But something changed it back again?'

'It was just a thought.'

'Explain yourself,' Sir Nicholas invited.

Antony picked up his glass, and now he gestured with it dangerously. 'I knew a girl who was so pure she could not say the word manure,' he remarked vaguely.

His uncle stared at him. 'What in heavens name do you mean?' he demanded. But to Antony's relief, before he was confronted with another request to explain the inexplicable, the door opened and Vera, followed by Jenny, burst into the room.

'Rush hour traffic's terrible,' she announced dramatically, 'but Jenny says I steer through it like a veteran. Ought to be proud of me, Nicholas.'

In the outburst of talk that followed, the subject of Edward Coke's libel action against his wife was momentarily shelved.

IV

Much later that same evening when Antony and Jenny, back in their own quarters, were beginning to think of going to bed, the telephone rang. Antony dragged himself out of his chair and went to answer it and was surprised to hear Desmond Barleycorn's voice. 'I thought we'd said all there was to say about this business, for tonight at least,' he greeted the solicitor on a note of protest.

'This is something new, something you've got to know about. Chief Inspector Sykes rang and asked me particularly to tell you.' Maitland was suddenly very still. 'You know that chap David Barrie?'

114

'Of course I know him.'

'He went to the theatre this evening and was stabbed and killed on his way home, walking through Avery Mews. I expect you know where that is.'

Maitland was silent for a moment. 'Not far from here,' he said at last. 'Not far from his father's house either. What I don't understand, Desmond, is who on earth could have wanted him dead.'

'I don't know, but Sykes was very insistent that I should tell you at once. Will you let Sir Nicholas know? I don't know how this will affect things tomorrow.'

'I expect Sykes phoned Bellerby himself, and Uncle Nick probably knows already. It's a bit late but I'll talk to him at breakfast time. We might get an adjournment out of it, if he agrees.'

And it wasn't until the following morning, when the phone rang while they were waiting for the kettle to boil, that he knew – this time from Detective Chief Inspector Sykes himself – that Elizabeth Coke was also dead.

PART THREE

Trinity Term, 1973

I

That took him downstairs, after the briefest word with
Jenny, to interrupt his uncle's first cup of coffee at an hour
when Sir Nicholas was not at all happy to be disturbed.
There followed a good deal of telephoning here and there,
an interval in court that entailed a good deal of explanation, Mr Justice Lovejoy being not a man easily convinced.
In fact they had to produce the Chief Inspector himself
before his lordship would consent to dismiss the case. Sir
Nicholas went back to chambers and Antony was about to
follow his example when Desmond stopped him, grabbing
his arm rather as a drowning man is reputed to clutch at a
straw. 'The police want to interview Edward,' he said.

'I imagine he knows his rights as well as you or I do. You
should be present, of course, and if there are any awkward
questions don't let him answer them. But it's possible that
it's a mere formality. After all, in the circumstances –' His
gesture embraced the whole courtroom and what had been
going on there.

'I know all that, but it's not my kind of thing at all,' said
Desmond. 'Neither was this, you know how I've relied on
you all the time. I'd be very much obliged if you'd come
back to the office with us and sit in on the interview.'

'I take it it's Chief Inspector Sykes who wants to see him.'

'Yes, and an Inspector Mayhew I think. Really I should
be grateful –'

'Don't worry, I'll come.' It had occurred to Maitland that
it might be interesting to find out a little more about the
two deaths. There was obviously a puzzle here, a striking

lack of motive, as it seemed to him just then.

'It's all right, Edward,' said Desmond, turning to his senior partner, who had been standing a little aloof from the conversation. 'He'll come.'

The offices of Messrs Coke, Coke and Barleycorn, Solicitors and Commissioners for Oaths, were of the old-fashioned kind, though they had departed from precedent so far as to have the windows cleaned, and Edward Coke's room at least was extremely comfortable. 'What time did Sykes say he'd get here?' asked Maitland, as Edward Coke waved him to a chair.

'About eleven,' said Edward. 'That's ten minutes from now,' he added unnecessarily, glancing at his watch. 'They should be here any minute, after all he was in court too.'

'He probably wants to have a cup of tea before he comes,' said Antony, grinning. 'He's a great man for a cup of tea is Sykes, and knows every place in London where it's possible to get one, whatever time of day it may be.'

'You sound as if you know him well.'

'Yes, I think you could say I do. We're by way of being friends. But if you're thinking,' he added hastily, 'that that might prejudice him in your favour I'd better put you right on that score. His superior is Chief Superintendent Briggs, and Briggs has no time for me at all.'

'I don't see that can make any difference either way,' said Edward. 'While we have a moment together, tell me. Elizabeth died before a verdict could be brought in the libel case. We were fighting what should have been a very private battle in as public a way as possible. Do you think the police could construe that into a motive for my killing her?'

'Do you want my honest opinion?'

'Of course I do, or I shouldn't have asked for it.'

'Well then, I think a good prosecutor, such as Bruce Halloran for instance, could make things sound very black indeed. We were going to lose that action, you know.'

'Yes, but this doesn't make things any better from my point of view. It just means that the accusation stands, and I'll never get the chance to refute it. Besides, though I admit to my shame that I was coming very near to hating Elizabeth, I didn't want her dead.'

'And David Barrie?'

'I just despised him.'

'All the same, if I were appearing for the prosecution there are two points I should make. One possible motive would be revenge; between them they'd gone a fair way towards ruining your life, hadn't they? There is also the fact that you've been at some pains to emphasise that you don't believe in divorce. From that point of view Elizabeth's death solves the problem for you, doesn't it?'

'Is that what you believe?'

'I didn't say so. I was putting a hypothetical case for the prosecution.'

'Well I can only say, as I said about this charge of perversion, there wouldn't be much point in obeying the church's law about divorce and going out and committing a much bigger sin.'

'The trouble is, the majority of the human race don't think reasonably, and why should you be the exception?'

'Is that what you believe?' asked Edward again.

'I'm here to help you ... remember?' said Antony. 'What were you doing yesterday evening?'

'I went straight home from the court. Desmond came with me and stayed long enough to have a drink, half an hour perhaps, and after that I was alone.'

'No visitors? No telephone calls made or received?'

'Nothing at all.'

'Well, that isn't much help. I wonder where Elizabeth died, and when for that matter. You didn't get that bit of information did you Desmond?'

'No, only about David, that he was killed on his way home from the theatre taking a short cut through Avery Mews. I take it it would be pretty quiet there at that time of night.'

'Very quiet indeed. I think I mentioned to you that a great many houses in our part of the world have been turned into offices. We'll have to see what information we can glean from Sykes.'

At that moment, as though on cue, the telephone rang to announce the Chief Inspector's arrival. Sykes was a square built man who always succeeded in looking as though he would be more comfortable in the country than in the town, and there was an air of placidity about him that Maitland had very rarely seen disturbed. Detective Inspector Mayhew, behind him, was slightly taller, very dark, a man whom Antony held in some regard and considered to have well earned his recent promotion. 'You here, Mr Maitland?' said Sykes, when he had greeted the other two men in his usual careful way. 'I can understand that Mr Coke might want his solicitor present –'

'In the circumstances –' Edward broke in, but Antony interrupted in his turn.

'Sheer curiosity on my part, Chief Inspector,' he said blandly. 'After all, I've seen a good deal of the two deceased in the last couple of days.'

'So you thought you'd pick my brains,' said Sykes good-humouredly. 'I don't know whether I've any information to give you.'

'Come now, you can't get away with that. What's sauce for the goose is sauce for the gander you know.'

'I suppose you mean by that,' said Sykes, 'that if I won't answer your questions your client won't answer mine.'

'Something of the sort.'

'It won't do, Mr Maitland, it won't do. It's every citizen's duty ... unless you're implying that to answer my

122

questions would in some way be to Mr Coke's disadvantage.'

'Nothing of the kind. Of course he'll tell you anything you want to know,' Antony assured him. 'At the same time I'm sure we could be of more help to your enquiries if we knew a little more of what happened.'

There came at that moment from Inspector Mayhew the rumbling sound that always reminded Antony of a grandfather clock about to strike, and that meant that Mayhew was about to speak. 'There may be something in what Mr Maitland says,' he remarked. 'And after all –'

'The evening papers will have the details,' said Sykes, completing the sentence for him. 'Very well, Mr Maitland, what is it you want to know?'

'We've been told that David Barrie was stabbed to death in Avery Mews as he returned from the theatre. Even that isn't very informative.'

'Then I'll try to improve on it.' Maitland was quite sure now that Sykes had intended all along to give him the particulars he wanted. He was also quite sure that the detective had his own reasons for so doing. 'Mr Barrie went straight home from the court, and we understand from the housekeeper that he was closeted after that for some time with his father. Then he left the house, banged out, she said, and that's all we know of his movements until he was found dead at ten-thirty. He'd apparently been stabbed repeatedly in the back, and the queer thing is that he was facing away from home as he fell, but of course there hasn't been time for a *post-mortem* examination yet.'

'It must have been a very short play.'

'That bit of information was given to you in error. It was the housekeeper who said he was going to the theatre, and he had a ticket for Jeremy Skelton's play "Done in by daggers" in his pocket, but it hadn't been used.'

'Well, I can understand that after what happened yesterday in court he wouldn't feel much like theatre-going. But

123

we'll come to that in a moment. What about Mrs Coke?'

'The odd thing is that she was found not far away, in Crocker Place.'

'But that's –'

'Exactly. That's where the Barries live. Another odd thing is that, although it's more frequented than Avery Mews, she wasn't found until the early hours of the morning. She had been stabbed a number of times too, and had fallen in the shadow of the steps that lead up to Number Twenty-three, so that any number of people may have passed and not noticed her there. Number Twenty-three is at the other end of the street from the Barries' house.'

'And had she been stabbed in the back too?'

'No, apparently the assailant had faced her. Again, of course, there's been no time for a *post-mortem* yet. We don't know which of them died first. And I don't need to tell you, Mr Maitland, we may never get a definite answer on that.'

'I see. Well, Chief Inspector, having satisfied our curiosity, what can we tell you?'

Sykes smiled at him. 'Mr Coke can start by telling me how he felt about the way the libel action was going,' he said.

'I thought it was going badly in spite of Mr Maitland's efforts,' said Edward. 'And I'm not blaming him, he had nothing to go on.'

'I've known him make bricks without straw before now,' said Sykes. Rather, thought Antony resentfully, as if he wasn't there at all.

'Well, I think he did that to a certain extent,' Edward explained. 'He did elicit the fact that Elizabeth wanted to marry again, which she'd been rather carefully trying to keep hidden.'

124

'But you think that would have made no difference to the verdict?'

'No difference at all. She had an explanation ready, and she's – I should say she was – an extremely convincing liar.'

'Why did you bring the libel action, Mr Coke?'

'I had no choice. My reputation . . . both professional and personal.'

'And why did you oppose Mrs Coke's desire for a divorce?'

'The judge agreed that had nothing to do with the libel action,' Maitland put in.

'No, Mr Maitland, we're not concerned with that now. This is a murder investigation,' Sykes reminded him.

'I opposed it,' said Edward, obviously only too eager to air his views on the subject, 'because I don't agree with divorce in any circumstances, and I'd have felt myself entirely in the wrong if I'd acquiesced.'

'And if Mrs Coke had succeeded, in spite of your endeavours, in gaining a verdict?'

'I should still have considered myself bound by the marriage.'

'Would you consider yourself a normal man with normal appetites, Mr Coke?'

Antony opened his mouth to speak but Edward stopped him with a gesture. 'It's what I've been trying to establish,' he said. 'If you're talking about sexual appetites.'

'That's exactly what I meant. How did you feel about the future?'

'I didn't want to face it alone,' Edward admitted.

'And now you're free. Have you anyone in view to share it with you?'

'I haven't had the right to consider such a thing.'

'Until this morning.'

125

'I must say what I said to Mr Maitland. I consider divorce a sin, but murder a much greater one.'

'And how do you feel about revenge?'

Edward smiled suddenly, so that for the moment his whole expression was lightened from its usual solemnity. 'You're a persistent man, Chief Inspector,' he said. 'I'd be lying if I told you I'd been thinking especially kindly about either Elizabeth or David Barrie, but I assure you my feelings didn't lead to my killing them.'

'Where were you last night, Mr Coke?'

'At home, alone. I have no alibi.'

'Very well then, we'll leave your affairs for the moment.'

'Don't you want to know what went on in court yesterday?' asked Edward, surprised.

'No, I've had a very good account from someone who was there. You may tell me one thing though, and since you're here, Mr Maitland, I'll include you in the question. Which was the truth, that Mrs Coke was proposing to marry David Barrie, or that she meant to accept his father?'

'I thought it would be David,' said Edward Coke rather hesitantly. 'I thought that, because it must have been how she persuaded him to back up her story. You haven't asked me whether it was true or not, Chief Inspector –'

'Whether it's true or otherwise isn't strictly relevant.'

'It's extremely relevant to me.'

'Yes, I can see it is, but you haven't answered my question, Mr Maitland,' he added, turning to Antony.

'I think she promised David marriage as the prize for his co-operation,' said Antony, 'but I'm also sure she promised to marry Owen Barrie, because he told me so himself. And my theory has been all along, Chief Inspector, that she was motivated in all she did by a desire for wealth. David could quite safely be cast off, after all; once the lie had been sworn to, he couldn't contradict Elizabeth without exposing himself to a charge of perjury.'

'That's very interesting,' said Sykes seriously. Mayhew was nodding his head but did not speak. 'Now I think you'll agree with me about two things, Mr Coke. First that these two murders must be connected –'

'That's obvious, isn't it?'

'Yes, I'm afraid it is. The second thing, however, you may not agree with quite so readily. It's that they must also be connected in some way with the situation between you and your wife.'

Edward took his time to glance at Maitland, and then at Desmond Barleycorn, and then back to the Chief Inspector again. 'I have to admit I find it as obvious as you do,' he said.

'Then perhaps you can tell me who might have had a motive, not just for killing Mrs Coke, but for killing David Barrie as well?'

'That's something I wish I could help you about,' said Edward sincerely. 'I quite see you think I'm the obvious person –'

'The Chief Inspector hasn't warned you, Mr Coke,' Antony put in.

'No, he hasn't, has he?' Edward sounded more surprised than pleased.

'My investigations are in a very early stage,' Sykes told them, 'and were delayed considerably by the necessity for attending court this morning. I'm sure you will all realise, gentlemen,' he added, looking round, 'that to question Mr Coke was the obvious beginning. I'm hoping, sir, that you may be able to tell me something about Mrs Coke's affairs, and who might have had a motive for killing her.'

'If you mean affairs in the sense of love affairs, Chief Inspector, I think by now you know as much about that as I do. But I admit I find the whole affair a puzzle, I can't think who would have done such a dreadful thing.'

'The friends who gave evidence in the libel action for instance.'

'Why should any of them have wanted to kill Elizabeth, let alone David Barrie as well?'

'Disillusionment,' said Inspector Mayhew suddenly.

'It doesn't make sense. Primrose believed her story, the Stowes believed her story. The Walpoles didn't, but they didn't hear it for the first time in court. Why should they suddenly be overcome with hatred?'

'And you can't think of anybody else?'

'Not a soul.'

'Very well then, Mr Coke, we'll leave it there. You realise I'm sure that I may have to talk to you again; as I said, the investigation is only just beginning. Are you coming our way, Mr Maitland?'

'Not as far as Scotland Yard, if that's what you mean,' said Antony, who had his own reasons for hating the place. 'But if Mr Coke doesn't need me any further –'

'I'm grateful for your help,' said Edward, 'and if I may echo what Chief Inspector Sykes said, I'm sure you realise that I may need your advice again.'

Desmond saw them out. 'No, Chief Inspector,' said Antony firmly as they reached the street, 'It's far too near lunchtime for me to want a cup of tea.'

'I know a little place just round the corner –' said Sykes insinuatingly.

'Yes, I'm sure you do. However, for this once, Chief Inspector, I think I must forgo the pleasure of your company.' He shared a grin between Sykes and Mayhew. 'It would be highly improper for me, let me remind you, to discuss a matter which a client of mine may be involved in.'

'Well, you see, Mr Maitland, it was an odd position,' said Mayhew. 'You and Sir Nicholas being in opposition. And knowing you as we do the Chief Inspector and I thought –'

'I know quite well what you thought, I ought to after all these years. You thought I had some private source of information, that perhaps might be of help to you.'

'Knowing you, Mr Maitland –' Sykes began, but Antony interrupted him ruthlessly.

'You said you had your own source of information about the libel action,' he said. 'I take it, then, it isn't matters of fact you want from me but matters of opinion.'

'I won't say you're wrong. Quite frankly, Mr Maitland, I can't see you taking a case like that if something hadn't convinced you that your client was telling the truth.'

'For that matter, have you ever known Uncle Nick take a divorce case before?'

'No, I must say I haven't.'

'Well then, something had convinced him that his client was in the right. Can't we just leave it at that in my case too?'

'Knowing you, Mr Maitland -'

'You said that before,' Antony reminded him. 'I have my own ideas about both Edward and Elizabeth Coke ... and about David Barrie for that matter. But they're no concern of yours.'

'There's one point we didn't put to your client,' said Sykes, not visibly downcast. 'He's a Roman Catholic, isn't he?'

'That, I'm sure, your informant concerning the libel action has told you.'

'Well – you'll put me right if I'm wrong about this, Mr Maitland – but it seems to me that the point he made concerning the difference in his eyes between remarrying and committing murder wasn't quite valid.'

For once in his life he had succeeded in astonishing Maitland. 'What on earth do you mean?' he asked.

'Well, as I understand it he could go to confession and have the murder wiped off the slate as it were. Whereas if it were a case of remarriage, he'd have to give his second wife up in order to put himself right with the church.' He

129

broke off staring as Maitland burst out laughing.

'I assure you it isn't quite as simple as that,' he said. 'You're correct enough about the second part of your statement, but if you've got the idea that a Catholic can do anything he likes provided he goes to confession afterwards, I'm afraid you've got another think coming.'

'I felt there might be some catch in it,' said Sykes soberly. 'Supposing you were defending him now, on a charge of murdering his wife, would you start objecting to the jurors if they weren't Catholics, as they might do in America, I understand?'

'May I remind you, Chief Inspector, that you said yourself you're in the early stages of the investigation? The question of my defending Edward Coke doesn't arise, I imagine.'

'Not yet,' said Sykes. It might be that there was a shade of regret in his tone.

'Well, if you feel like that you ought to have warned him,' Antony retorted. 'In any case, I think the matter might be quite easily explained to the jury without resorting to those sort of tactics.' But he was thinking as he turned away a moment later that he wouldn't give you twopence for the collective intelligence of any jury; and in this it is to be regretted his feeling differed in no way from those of most of his brethren.

II

Sir Nicholas seemed to have been swallowed alive by the work that was awaiting him in chambers, and it wasn't until he and Vera came upstairs that evening after dinner that there was any chance of further talk. 'Thank goodness at least,' he said, sinking into his usual chair, 'there's no longer a ban on a little frank discussion of the situation.

I've found these last two weeks very trying, Antony.'

'I thought I was the only one to suffer,' said Antony, pouring brandy for his guests. (Since her marriage Vera had acquired a very gentlemanly taste in drinks.)

'By no means,' said his uncle, accepting the glass. Then he added, giving his nephew rather a keen look, 'Where did you disappear to when the court adjourned?'

'Desmond Barleycorn wanted me to be present when the police interviewed Edward Coke.'

'That was no part of your commitment to him.'

'Of course not. Sykes raised his eyebrows at my being there, but you know as well as I do, Uncle Nick, those two may be solicitors but their entire practice is a family one. As far as a criminal case is concerned they're a couple of innocents.'

'That is hardly the word I should have applied to your client,' said Sir Nicholas coldly. 'I mean of course Edward Coke, it hardly seems suitable to refer to him as the lay client in the circumstances.'

'Well, we agreed to differ about that. And honestly, Uncle Nick, no matter what you think of his character I can't see the faintest reason for him having added murder to the other things you think he's guilty of.'

'Revenge,' said Vera in her deep voice.

'Yes, I suppose that's the most valid motive, but I think myself he was still clinging to the hope that during the course of the divorce action the truth might come out, even though we were all pretty sure we'd lose the libel case.'

'Stubborn to the last,' Sir Nicholas commented. 'What had he to tell Sykes?'

'That he hadn't an alibi and that he didn't know anybody with a motive for either or both of the murders,' said Antony succinctly. 'No warning was issued, Sykes was very insistent that the investigations were only just beginning.'

'But I suppose if he is accused eventually you'll defend him?'

'I suppose I will. But that doesn't mean I've made up my mind –'

'Haven't you?'

'No. Sykes made two points, that the murders were obviously connected, and that they were equally obviously connected with the libel action. That puts Edward Coke right in the middle of things, I'm afraid, but I honestly haven't made up my mind either way.'

'I don't think even you can think of anyone else who might have done the killing.'

'That's all you know, Uncle Nick,' said Jenny, who had been talking to her husband before dinner. 'Antony thinks –'

'If I am to be edified by his views,' said Sir Nicholas, who had come upstairs with every intention of hearing them, 'I should prefer to have them from his own lips.'

Jenny subsided with a grin in Vera's direction. Antony said idly, 'What about Primrose Ross?'

'I should hardly imagine that stabbing a man to death – or a woman either – would be much in her line.'

'I haven't told you yet what Sykes had to say about the murders,' said Antony, and proceeded to do so.

'Why does that make Miss Ross's guilt more likely?' asked Sir Nicholas when he had finished.

'Not more likely perhaps, but at least possible,' said Antony. 'As I see it, David Barrie was upset by what had been said in court –'

'I think Mrs Coke explained the position very well, and she denied absolutely, if you remember, that there was anything between her and Mr Owen Barrie.'

'Yes, I remember. I also know what he told me. I think David went home and had it out with his father, and what he heard upset him so that he went wandering around the streets instead of going to see "Done in by daggers" like a sensible man. And wherever he went it was a short cut to come home through Avery Mews, and I think he met the murderer there.'

'So much seems obvious.'

'Yes, but – I told you this, Uncle Nick – he was facing away from home when he fell. The murderer may have threatened him so that he turned to run away and was stabbed in the back, or he or she may have made up some tale to persuade him to retrace his steps, with the same final result. As for Elizabeth, the murderer faced her apparently, but that would have been just woman to woman, nothing impossible.'

'And how did Miss Ross know the whereabouts of these people?'

'That's rather a difficulty whoever did it. For the moment we might postulate that the murderer followed Elizabeth, and merely chanced upon David when leaving the scene of the crime.'

'And the motive for all this in Miss Ross's case?'

'Disillusionment,' said Vera before Antony could speak. 'Plain as the nose on your face.'

'You are not, I hope, postulating an unnatural connection between the two women,' said Sir Nicholas. 'That, my dear, I think is out of the question.'

'Yes, I think so too,' said Antony before Vera could speak. 'But I do think Primrose had a crush on her, rather as a schoolgirl might have on a favourite mistress. That might have very much the same effect, mightn't it, Jenny?'

'I think it might,' said Jenny slowly. 'I haven't seen this Miss Ross, of course, but it would seem to be rather a violent reaction if she really killed two people because of it.'

'Yes, I think so too. But she isn't my only candidate, Uncle Nick.'

'Who else?' asked his uncle in a resigned tone.

'My instructing solicitor, Desmond Barleycorn.'

'Oh, for heavens sake! Really, Antony, this is too much. Was he disillusioned too?'

'Not a bit of it, just the opposite in fact. He's very violently on Edward Coke's side, and it's just possible that the prospect of losing the case coupled with the evidence of David and Elizabeth's duplicity might have driven him to violence.'

'You don't really believe that?' said Vera accusingly.

'No, I don't, because I like him, as a matter of fact. But we were discussing possibilities,' said Antony apologetically.

'Well,' said Sir Nicholas in a grumbling tone, 'you've told us how you think David Barrie came to be in Avery Mews when he was stabbed. What about Mrs Coke? What was she doing in this part of the world? Her hotel is at the other side of the park.'

'That brings me to my third possibility,' said Antony, 'and I don't like contemplating this one either. I think she had been visiting Owen Barrie.'

'You'd better explain that.'

'Yes, I'm going to. I think she hoped to get in first with her story of what had been said in court, before David could do so. He'd already talked to his father, as we know, and I imagine the matter had been thrashed out between them, because my question to David in court, if you remember Uncle Nick, completely flabbergasted him.'

'Wait a bit! If Mrs Coke lied a second time, in denying any promise of marriage to Owen Barrie, but confirming that she wanted to marry David to put matters right as she put it –'

He broke off there and Antony said encouragingly, 'That's right, Uncle Nick. It makes it all the more likely that she was lying all the time, and confirms my theory – don't you think? – that her whole motive was gain.'

'I suppose it does,' said his uncle. 'I suppose too that her talk with Owen Barrie could hardly have been amicable. Is that what you're getting at? That Barrie followed her from his house and killed her?'

'I told you I hadn't made up my mind about Edward Coke's guilt or innocence,' said Antony. 'I'm still less sure about this, but I do think it's a possibility, and perhaps more of a possibility than that Edward killed his wife.'

There followed a rather stunned silence. Jenny got up and poured a little more cognac into Sir Nicholas's glass, he seemed to have disposed of a first helping rather absent-mindedly. 'You know what he's telling us, my dear,' Sir Nicholas appealed to his wife after a moment. 'He's saying that if Edward Coke is arrested and he's briefed for the defence he'll indulge in his usual meddlesome tactics. Above and beyond the call of duty,' he added bitterly.

'But if you think Mr Coke is guilty, Uncle Nick,' Jenny pointed out, 'that shouldn't matter. At least it won't mean somebody else is gunning for Antony.'

Sir Nicholas closed his eyes and appeared to swoon. 'From you at least, Jenny, I'd expected a greater appreciation of the English language,' he said. But he did not add the thought that was in both his and Vera's mind, that Maitland had been known to be right on occasion. Though Vera, who'd profited from his help in her professional days, would have been inclined to put the matter more forcefully.

They were completely in accord, however, about a deeper, though so far vague uneasiness about where their nephew's unconventional ways might lead him.

Tuesday, 26th June

I

After that the matter was by common consent dismissed as a topic of conversation in Kempenfeldt Square, though Antony couldn't help his mind going back occasionally to the problem of Edward Coke's guilt or innocence, and to wondering how Chief Inspector Sykes and Inspector Mayhew were getting on with their enquiries. So he wasn't particularly surprised the following Tuesday morning when his study of a particularly intricate contract was interrupted by the telephone, and picking up the receiver he heard Hill's voice saying apologetically, 'There's Mr Barleycorn asking to speak to you, Mr Maitland. Shall I send him in?'

'Yes certainly, Hill.' No-one had ever discovered the full extent of Hill's sensitivity, because there was a general belief in chambers that he had been born apologising, and consequently no-one had ever said anything that could even remotely sound like a reproof. A few moments later Willett, in his usual bouncy way, was ushering the visitor into Maitland's narrow room. John Willett, unofficial second-in-command to old Mr Mallory in the clerk's office, had always taken a particular and sympathetic interest in Maitland's affairs. Now he grimaced at him over the visitor's shoulder as Desmond passed him and went towards the desk; a complicated sort of grimace that Antony couldn't fathom at all. But perhaps it was intended as a warning of some kind.

'I expect you're surprised to see me,' said Desmond, seating himself when their greetings were over. Willett had

136

gone now and the door had closed gently behind him. 'Something rather awkward has come up.'

To say he had been half expecting the visit would perhaps not be tactful. Antony compromised by murmuring something about always being pleased to see his visitor, and waiting for him to come to the point, which he seemed strangely reluctant to do.

'I know I ought to have talked to your clerk first,' said Desmond, 'but in the particular circumstances ... well you'll see what I mean when I explain. You know the police – that man Sykes who seemed to be a friend of yours – said they were just beginning their investigations. Well, over the weekend they seem to have been pretty busy.'

'I see,' said Maitland and was never more wrong in his life.

'They've interviewed Owen Barrie twice,' said Desmond, 'and the second time they warned him. It was after that that he called me.'

'Naturally,' said Antony, concealing his surprise.

'Yes, I suppose ... but it isn't our line of country at all, any more than the libel action was. And I thought we'd lost Owen as a client altogether over that affair, but since he's come to us I couldn't think of anything else to do but ask your help.'

'I take it we're talking about the murders of Mrs Coke and of David Barrie?'

'Yes, of course we are.'

'You must forgive me for mentioning it, but in that respect I consider myself to some degree committed to Edward Coke's interests.'

'But Edward doesn't need your help now,' said Desmond with a rather wild look.

'I'm relieved to hear it.'

'Is that what you thought when your clerk announced me? That it was about Edward?'

'Well, of course it was,' said Antony rather impatiently. 'For one thing ... does Owen Barrie know you're here?'

'Yes, it was he who particularly suggested that I should get in touch with you.'

'That does surprise me. I liked him, you know, when we talked together, but we didn't exactly agree on all subjects. Look here, perhaps you'd better tell me how all this arose.'

'Owen phoned Edward and Edward called me in straight away because of course – though we've always been Mr Barrie's solicitors, at least Edward's father was in the beginning – he couldn't possibly act in the matter of someone accused of murdering his own wife. But we talked it over and decided there was nothing improper in my taking on the case. I admit I wouldn't have agreed, not feeling myself particularly competent in the criminal line, if it hadn't been for Owen's suggestion that I should ask you to act. I know you'll keep me on the right lines,' he added ingenuously.

'That's all very well, and you say you discussed with Mr Coke the possibility of your taking the case and he agreed. Does he know you're approaching me?'

'Yes, he thought it was a very good idea. If he doesn't object, I don't see why you should.'

'Possible conflict of interest,' Antony explained.

Desmond recoiled a little. 'Are you telling me that you think Edward is guilty?' he demanded.

'No, of course not.' No need to explain his ambivalence on the subject. 'But as Mr Coke's solicitor, Desmond, it's only fair I should put all the possibilities before you. Suppose we defend Owen Barrie – also supposing they do in fact arrest him – and get him off. There are two possibilities then, the police may still be quite convinced they were right and call it a day, or they may entertain some doubts and start casting around for another suspect. That

138

might bring them round full circle to Edward Coke again.'

'He didn't do it.'

'That isn't the point.'

Desmond thought about it for a while. 'If it did come to that you could then undertake Edward's defence,' he pointed out at last.

'True, but –'

'Mr Maitland, I've read most of your cases,' said Desmond eagerly. 'You believe that the best form of defence is to prove that someone else committed the crime, don't you?'

Maitland scowled at that remark for a moment, but then his face cleared. 'Something like that,' he admitted.

'And you're thinking that perhaps, if you undertake Owen Barrie's defence, you may discover that Edward is really the guilty party? No you needn't answer that, I can see it's an awkward question, but there's nothing for it now but completely plain speaking. I trust Edward absolutely and I'm quite sure nothing like that could happen, and in spite of your doubts I still ask you to take the case.'

'That's a pretty good recommendation,' said Antony smiling. 'Would you be prepared to explain my reluctance to Mr Coke and see what he says about it?'

'Yes, if you want me to.'

'I'd like to take the case,' said Maitland slowly. 'Partly because I'm curious, and partly because I don't like unfinished business.'

'What exactly do you mean by that?'

'That my efforts over the libel suit left Edward Coke exactly where he was before, with his reputation badly tarnished. If I agree to represent Mr Barrie, and if he really is arrested, he'd be my first concern of course and I'd do everything I could for him. But there's always the chance that something might turn up to prove that Mr Coke's story about his marriage was the true one. And that I *do* believe,' he added, smiling at his companion.

'I say, that is good news.'

'Don't get carried away. I'm not promising a thing, you know, only that a possibility exists. And while we're talking, Desmond, may I ask you what your opinion is about Owen Barrie's guilt or innocence?'

'I haven't seen him yet, I thought if you agreed we could do so together. Thinking it over I do see that if Edward is out of it Owen's the next most likely suspect, because obviously, as I think we said when we talked before, the deaths must be connected somehow with the libel action. So I haven't really made up my mind either way, but if he did do it I rather sympathise with him and I'd like to do my best for him.'

'Fair enough. Go back to your office, Desmond, and talk to your partner, and be sure you don't gloss over anything I've said. Then, if Mr Coke agrees, you can get in touch with Mallory, and we'll arrange a conference with Owen Barrie.'

'I'm pretty sure Edward will agree, and I think we ought to see Owen as soon as possible,' said Desmond. 'Could you possibly make it this afternoon?'

Maitland glanced at the papers he was perusing. 'Make it after four o'clock and I'm your man,' he said, carefully keeping any hint of resignation out of his voice. 'The important thing is to make Edward Coke understand.'

'Yes, I quite see that. Trust me,' said Desmond, and disappeared so rapidly that he went without the formality of a farewell.

II

It was fortunate for Maitland that, except on rare occasions, he had the gift of concentration. After Desmond had gone he dismissed the whole matter of the murders from his mind, and went back to the breach of contract, which was precisely the kind of case he disliked most. Presumably some fellow lawyer had drawn the thing up, there was the name on the outside in fact for anyone to see, otherwise as he told his uncle at lunchtime he'd be very much inclined to suspect diabolical intervention. He also told Sir Nicholas about Owen Barrie's unexpected request, and exactly what had passed between himself and Desmond Barleycorn on the subject.

'Very proper,' said Sir Nicholas approvingly. 'If I were a betting man, Antony, I'd wager a small sum that you will hear no more of the matter. In view of what you've said, Edward Coke won't agree.'

But there he was wrong. When he got back to chambers Maitland found a message waiting for him that Mr Barleycorn and Mr Barrie would call upon him sometime between a quarter and half past four. 'Be on your guard,' said Sir Nicholas in a tone full of foreboding, and went so far as to follow his nephew down the corridor to his own room to repeat the warning. 'The fellow's up to something,' he added.

'Why should you think that, Uncle Nick?'

'I should have thought it would be obvious even to you that one of them must have done it,' said Sir Nicholas positively.

'I don't even know yet how Barrie wants to plead,' Antony expostulated. 'It may be quite obvious that he's guilty, you know we'd already discussed the possibility, and then all we can do is present the matters in the best light we can.'

'Well, don't present them in such a good light that the police start looking elsewhere,' his uncle remonstrated. 'There's every possibility you'll have Edward Coke after you with a hatchet if you do.'

'Come now, Uncle Nick, it's not as bad as that. I gave him every opportunity to turn the matter over to somebody else, you admitted that yourself.'

'We'll see who's right,' said his uncle ominously; and went back to his own room, still most likely, thought his nephew undutifully, prophesying doom.

Knowing Desmond's ways to some extent by now Antony pushed his papers aside and provided himself with a fresh note pad at four o'clock precisely, and true to his expectations the phone rang announcing the visitors no more than three seconds after he had completed his preparations. This time he only saw Willett for a second as the visitors surged past him, Desmond in his usual eager way, Owen Barrie more ponderously. 'I think I should say I'm grateful to you for seeing me, Mr Maitland,' said Barrie coming to a halt by the desk. 'When we last met there were things we didn't see eye to eye about, but I've been forced to change my opinion since then.'

'Sit down, Mr Barrie, and don't think any more about that.' He was shocked by the other man's appearance. All the ruddiness had gone from his complexion and in some way he seemed to have shrunk. Desmond pulled one of the visitors' chairs up behind his client, which was just as well because Barrie's legs seemed to give way at that moment and he sank back into it rather heavily. The solicitor then took a seat himself, and looked expectantly at Maitland, obviously waiting for him to take the proceedings into his own hands. And that, thought Antony, is the result of his experience of me already, so I shouldn't be surprised.

'Willett will be bringing us tea in a moment,' he said. 'But if you'd like something stronger, Mr Barrie, I can arrange for that. You look a bit done in.'

'Tea will be fine,' said Owen Barrie. 'And if I look done in as you call it, Mr Maitland, you're to some extent to blame.'

'I am?' asked Antony startled.

'For asking the question in court that started the whole thing,' said Barrie.

'If you feel like that about it I regard your being here as extremely magnanimous,' said Antony, trying by his tone to inject a slightly lighter note into the proceedings.

'On the contrary, I consider myself indebted to you. It opened my eyes, Mr Maitland, and it's better to see clearly than to go through life blindfold . . . however much it hurts. When David told me –'

'Wait a bit! Before we start there are a few things we ought to get clear.'

Willett came at that moment with the tea, and there was a pause while it was distributed. When he had gone again, 'What exactly are these things you want to get clear, Mr Maitland?' Barrie asked.

'Exactly what you want of me for one thing.'

'I thought perhaps Desmond had made that clear.'

'Yes, but there are one or two questions to which I don't think he knows the answers. He said, for instance, that the police had been to see you.'

'Yes, the first time, of course, on Friday. A matter of routine they said, and I could well believe that. But then they came again yesterday evening, and before they started on the questions they issued what I believe is known as the usual warning. And as the questioning went on I could see my answers didn't satisfy them. I began to be worried, and so first thing this morning I phoned Edward.'

'Having, I suppose, answered every question the police put to you on both occasions.'

'Yes, of course. It was my duty to co-operate, wasn't it? Why shouldn't I answer their questions?'

'Because by doing so and only then calling your solicitor you may be guilty of shutting the stable door after the horse has gone. However, it brings us to the heart of the matter, Mr Barrie. You are in some apprehension that

143

following this latest bout of questioning your arrest for murder may follow?'

'It seems logical, from Chief Inspector Sykes's attitude ... I've nothing to complain of, you know, they were both perfectly polite, in fact I should say that the Chief Inspector is rather a gentle man.

Maitland had a grin for that. 'Would you though? I must tell him that some time. So what you want, Mr Barrie, is that I should represent you if the case comes to trial. If it's merely more questioning, of course, Mr Barleycorn's presence would be sufficient safeguard.'

'You know perfectly well –' Desmond began.

'In the circumstances, Mr Barrie has described to us, Desmond, I rather gather he has already told the police everything they want to know. So the next question is, Mr Barrie, how would you want to plead?'

That brought a silence. 'I didn't kill Elizabeth and I didn't kill my son,' said Owen Barrie steadily. 'The plea would be not guilty, of course.'

'I'm under the impression that the question of motive plays a good part in the police's suspicions ... if, indeed you're right about that.'

'That's my impression too.'

'Then I should be failing in my duty if I didn't point out to you that where a crime had been committed under intolerable pressure a plea of guilty to a lesser charge will sometimes be accepted by the Court.'

Owen waited with obvious impatience for him to finish. 'I will not plead guilty to something I didn't do, Mr Maitland. I understand your position, but I should be glad if you will regard my answer as final,' he said then, with a touch of frost in his voice.

'Thank you, that's all I wanted to know.'

'All?' said Owen, frowning.

'I meant before we get started, Mr Barrie. Murder is an

unpleasant business, and among the questions I shall be putting to you there may be a good many that you won't like.'

'I can see I shall have to put up with that.'

'I shall be grateful for your tolerance,' said Maitland formally. 'I think the best thing would be if you would tell us what has been happening, starting when your son David got back from court on Thursday afternoon.'

'He came in in a rage. I was already at home. You know, Mr Maitland, from our previous conversation that the outcome of the libel action was of particular interest to me. Anyway, I was in my study. I wasn't surprised when David came in because he knew of my interest, but I *was* surprised by the way he looked. Almost as if he hated me. But he took his time to close the door behind him, and then he said almost viciously, "That bloody man Maitland," – forgive me, I'm quoting – "says Elizabeth had promised to marry you." '

'I see,' said Maitland slowly. 'What did you do then?'

'I persuaded him to come and sit down and brought him some scotch, almost neat. He looked as if he needed it. And then I told him, choosing my words rather carefully because he was in a dreadful state, that Elizabeth and I were indeed going to be married when her divorce was made final, and that I had only kept it from him because of my promise to her. She felt it would be improper to mention the matter – I told you all this before, Mr Maitland – until she was a free woman. And he listened to me quite quietly, sipping his whisky, and then he put his glass down on the table behind him and looked up at me, and again there was that naked hatred in his eyes. "Why do you think I agreed to back her up in this preposterous story?" he asked.'

There was a silence there, but this was no time for an interruption. Desmond, in fact, seemed to be holding his breath, because he expelled it after a moment in a rather noisy sigh. 'I couldn't even then believe what he was telling me,' Owen said. 'I said to him, "Because it was true, of course. Elizabeth explained it all to me, how it happened, how she couldn't help it. I didn't blame her." "No, I suppose you reserved all the blame for me," David said, "so now I'll tell you there wasn't a word of truth in this story your lady love told you. She got my backing by promising to marry me, I'd been in love with her for months, you know, but if I back out now and tell the truth I expect I'll be had up for perjury." '

'Did he tell you – I said some of my questions would be distressing Mr Barrie – whether he had had intercourse with Mrs Coke during this time he said he had been in love with her?'

'Yes. It was very odd, Mr Maitland, he boasted about it and yet at the same time he was ashamed.'

'And when had the – I can only call it a plot – been laid?'

'Every bit of six months ago so far as I could gather. Even then they'd been seeing each other for a few months, so of course it wasn't hard for him to believe, when Elizabeth told him she wanted a quick divorce, that it was because she wanted to marry him.'

'Who suggested the means of getting the divorce?'

'David said that was Elizabeth herself. He said she'd got it all off pat, she'd been reading up law books somewhere, I don't know where.'

'I expect her husband had a number in his study at home.'

'Yes, that would be it no doubt. Anyway, that was when David started to visit Elizabeth and Edward when there were just the three of them present. It was to back up the story they were to tell in court later. I don't think David had bargained for the libel action, but he says Elizabeth told him it was just part of the same bargain, if they won – I should say if she won, I suppose – it would be as good as having the divorce petition granted, that would go through without any further bother.'

'I see. And your reaction to all this, Mr Barrie?'

'Horror, disbelief, but finally I knew it must be true.'

'Even though you knew that David had committed perjury, both in what he said about Edward Coke and by saying that Mrs Coke was not in love with him?'

'He may be telling the truth about that last point without knowing it,' said Barrie sadly. 'But I can't deny the intent was there. Only I still maintain he wouldn't lie to me. He wouldn't – he wouldn't think it was worth it.'

'I see,' said Antony again. There was no doubt that the admission cost Owen a good deal. 'I'm sorry,' Maitland added lamely. 'So you believe the story David told you that evening?'

'I have no choice.'

'What happened then?'

'I tried to comfort him in the only way I knew, by telling him that I myself had been equally taken in. I don't think it helped him at all to know we'd both been made fools of, any more than it did me.'

'You were completely disillusioned about Mrs Coke, then?'

'Naturally I was. I realised the bitter wrong that had been done to Edward, and the woman who would do a thing like that . . . I thought myself very deeply in love, Mr Maitland, I think you know that. But David's story finished that absolutely.'

'Yes, I understand that. And then?'

'I began to be worried about the perjury angle, for David's sake, I mean. So I asked him what had been the reaction in court when you asked your question. He'd already told me he blurted out that he was engaged to her himself. And he told me there was nothing to worry about,

about that. She'd explained to the court her reasons for keeping silent about their engagement, and that those reasons applied to him too. Any action could only be because they had both denied that she was in love with him, and he felt that she was quite capable of making any jury sympathetic towards that point of view. And then he said, "You're going to shop us then?" I suppose he meant, give them away, because of what he'd told me that evening. I knew it was my duty to do so, but I couldn't say so right out. I only said I'd think about it. But, of course, later in the evening when I did think it out I could see Edward's predicament only too clearly, and I realised I couldn't remain silent.'

'So then –?'

'I asked David to remain quietly at home with me that evening. He wasn't in a fit state to go roaming around, and quite honestly I was afraid of what he might do.'

'To Elizabeth Coke, you mean?'

'Yes, that's exactly what I do mean. He was furious about being deceived, and even more furious that she had never meant to keep her word. And I think his love for her had gone very deep.'

'But he went out after all?'

'Yes. I knew he had a ticket for this thriller everyone's talking about, and he was going to meet some of his friends there, but he went out much too early for that. So I consoled myself with the thought that perhaps if he walked around a bit he'd cool off, and might even see things in a clearer light. And I was glad, I must admit, to be alone for a while, because I had a lot to think about too.'

'Does your housekeeper live in?'

'No, she puts my dinner on the table, and then goes home. The arrangement is that she'll clear away in the morning, but I usually put things tidy for her if I'm alone, or if only David's in. So at eight o'clock I sat down to my dinner, and by five past, I suppose, I heard the front door close and knew I was alone. I went back to my room when I'd finished and tried to read, and then at half past nine I heard the door bell.' He paused and looked rather sharply at Maitland. 'You were expecting that, Mr Maitland,' he said almost accusingly.

'Let's just say I wasn't surprised. For one thing, what was Mrs Coke doing in your street that evening? For another, I couldn't see her not attempting some sort of explanation to you in the hopes of a reconciliation.'

'Well that first point is exactly the thing that brought the police to my doorstep a second time I think,' said Owen. 'I suppose it was obvious she was either coming or going to my place. I didn't really want to let her in, but she said something like, "After all we've been to each other, Owen," and I was afraid she'd make a scene on the doorstep. So I stood back and let her pass.'

'I think perhaps you can understand, Mr Barrie, that at this point your story gets extraordinarily interesting to us. I'm correct in surmising, am I not, that you have told all this to the police?'

'I don't tell lies, Mr Maitland.'

'There was no such insinuation intended. It is not always wise however, or even necessary, to tell the whole truth.'

'I didn't see any reason not to tell them. I think you can imagine my emotions when they first visited me, Mr Maitland. If I felt Elizabeth had got no more than she deserved, there was still David. I suppose a stranger might say the same thing about him, but he was my son. Anything I could do to help, anything at all . . . though I agree I didn't realise where it was leading me.'

'And on their second visit?'

'We went over everything again in much greater detail. I don't say they were trying to trip me up, but certainly the repeated questions would have had that effect if I hadn't been telling the truth.'

'Well, as I said, I must know, as Mr Barleycorn must know, every single thing you told them. Perhaps you'll continue your story bearing that in mind.'

'I'm doing my best,' Owen protested. 'And this is . . . even more embarrassing than what went before.'

Antony smiled at him. 'That's exactly why I'm stressing the point, Mr Barrie,' he said. 'It couldn't have been otherwise.'

'I suppose not. Anyway, she came in, and we went into my study which is where I had been sitting. Since my wife died the drawing room seems strangely lonely, and even before David's death he didn't often stay in with me in the evening. I think Elizabeth hoped David hadn't been home yet, hadn't talked to me, because she started by saying, "Owen darling something dreadful happened in court today, something I'm afraid you'll misunderstand when you hear about it." '

'What did you say in reply to that?'

'I told her that David had come straight home from court, and told me everything. She didn't understand at first, or pretended not to, just told me that she'd only kept silent about our love for each other because she wanted to protect me, to keep me out of this terrible affair. So then I told her again, quite bluntly, that David had told me everything. About the lies they had both told, and the fact that she had given him her promise of eventual marriage if he would perjure himself for her sake.'

'I imagine that shook her, didn't it?' asked Maitland, not without some satisfaction in his voice.

'Yes it did, quite visibly. But all the same she embarked on a sort of an explanation. She said everything they told the court was true, that Edward was a pervert just as she had told me, but that she had had to make that promise to

David to get his backing. She said it was for our sake, that I think was the worst thing of all. I told her quite flatly I didn't believe her. She cried a little, and even fell on her knees and said again, "After all we've been to each other." But I could see now that it was obviously insincere. I was only ashamed that she'd ever taken me in.'

'And what *had* you been to each other, Mr Barrie?'

'There was a promise of marriage between us when she was free. She confided in me, as I thought, things that she couldn't tell to anybody else. But I imagine you're referring to a sexual relationship. I'm no better than the next man, if she'd given me the slightest encouragement . . . but she always said our love was too pure for us to need to give one another any further proof of sincerity.'

'I knew it!' said Maitland. 'It was that damned sancti-monious attitude that convinced me in the first place,' he added to Desmond. 'And when I say convinced me, I believed Edward Coke before, but sometimes a few doubts would creep in.'

'But even Mr Barrie believes in Edward now,' said Desmond, 'and his story will clear him completely, won't it? I mean –'

'It's only too obvious what you mean,' said Maitland a little dryly. 'Mr Barrie, you think you're going to be arrested, or you wouldn't have wanted to see me.'

'That's right.'

'How imminent do you think it is?'

'I'd be surprised if they held their hands much longer.'

'Yes, well, we'll go into that in a moment. Meanwhile, Desmond, if you're thinking of getting our client to make a statement to the press exonerating Edward, it won't do. If Mr Barrie is arrested they wouldn't dare print it for fear of contempt of court, and in any case the story will go down much better with the jury told in his own words and in his own way.'

151

'Yes, I see that of course, I'm sorry,' said Desmond, a little downcast. 'All the same –'

'At the moment Mr Barrie is our first concern ... remember? Let's finish first with Elizabeth's visit to you, Mr Barrie. How long did she stay?'

'It must have been quite half an hour, perhaps a little longer. I was upset, I think you can imagine that, I didn't look at the clock.'

'Let's say she left your house at ten past ten. Did you go with her to the door?'

'Yes. Frankly I wanted to make quite sure she was off the premises. The whole thing revolted me and I just wanted it to be over.'

'Was anyone about in Crocker Place at that time?'

'I didn't see a soul. Most of the houses are places of business now, you know.'

'But someone could have been there, if they were anxious not to show themselves?'

'Oh, quite easily. Each house has six steps up to the front door, and they cast a shadow. That's how Elizabeth wasn't found until the early hours of the morning.'

'Have the police said anything to you about the time of death?'

'No, but they seemed to be assuming that it had happened immediately after she left me.'

'How long did you stand at the door?'

'A moment or two, no more.'

'And there might have been someone in the street, perhaps even somebody standing in the shadow of the steps of the house opposite?'

'Certainly, I wasn't looking for anything of the kind.'

'I see. Motive isn't supposed to count in a court of law, and I dare say you know that, Mr Barrie; but the sad fact is that it's one of the most telling points the prosecution can make, and in this case even the rawest junior among treasury counsel could convince the jury that you had it and had it in abundance. There is also opportunity. If you're arrested it will be for Elizabeth Coke's murder, I presume. How would anybody but you have known that she was there and at that particular time? Which brings us to the question, which can't be left out of it altogether, did David make a habit of walking through Avery Mews?'

'He did and I'm afraid I can't deny knowledge of the fact. He was always recommending it to our neighbours as a short cut.'

Maitland smiled at him again. 'You don't make things any easier for us, do you, Mr Barrie?' he asked. 'Did you add to your other indiscretions, I wonder, by allowing the police to put all these things down in the form of a statement and signing it?'

For the first time Barrie looked somewhat abashed. 'I'm afraid I did,' he admitted.

'Before or after you were warned?'

'After. I still wanted to help them and do anything to catch David's killer, you know, and I'm afraid I was naive enough to think that as I was telling the truth there could be no harm in it.'

'Yet your first instinct after they had gone was to call Edward Coke.'

'I slept on it first, though I admit I called rather early this morning.'

'What is your attitude towards him now?'

'They were lying about him, Elizabeth and David. I'm just sorry I ever misjudged him.'

'Was that your only reason for consulting him, as a sort of apology?'

'Not at all. I've always dealt with your firm, Desmond, though of course it was with Edward's father for the most part while he was alive.'

'They have not, however a criminal practice.'

153

'No, I know that, but I had you in mind, Mr Maitland. Desmond will bear me out about that. You impressed me very much when you came to see me, even though at that time I didn't agree with your point of view. I'm sure if anyone can help me you can.'

'Well, until there's an arrest and we hear the prosecution case put on in the Magistrate's Court we don't know in detail what they've got against you, except these two points of motive and opportunity that I've mentioned. Thinking back to your last talk with Chief Inspector Sykes and Inspector Mayhew, Mr Barrie, can you think of anything else they may be holding against you, was there any hint of some further evidence?'

'They asked a lot of questions about knives.'

'Good God in heaven,' said Maitland, startled. 'What about them?'

'They said the same knife had been used on both occasions,' said Owen Barrie, speaking with difficulty now. 'They spoke of a rather triangular blade coming to a point and very sharp, the kind of thing you might find in any kitchen they said, and wondered if we might have something of the sort in ours.'

'Yes, I know,' said Maitland rather grimly, 'all very innocent.'

'Well, I couldn't see any harm in letting them look. As a matter of fact I knew there was a set of knives in a rack, matching though all different sizes, but I knew I hadn't taken one of them and ... well! So I took Sykes and Mayhew down to the kitchen to look.'

'This was yesterday evening, you say. Had your housekeeper left?'

'Yes, she had, but she told me at lunch time today that they'd been back talking to her. The trouble was, you see, that one of the knives was missing from that set, the middle one, and though I showed them the cutlery drawer

and let them rummage about just as they liked it didn't
come to light. So they came back to ask Mrs Hill if she'd put
it anywhere special for any reason.'

'And had she?'

'No, but she said she'd used it yesterday when cutting up
steak for a casserole. And she said she'd drawn it for them,
and the younger one had drawn his breath in rather
sharply when he saw what it looked like. And she couldn't
remember putting it away, because it's so much a matter of
habit with her that she might have done it quite uncon-
sciously. Or not done it at all of course.'

'Was that all her evidence?'

'She said they'd shown her a piece of paper which they
said was a warrant – a lot of legal stuff, she said, which she
didn't bother to read – and they called two men in to go
through the place thoroughly from top to bottom I gather.'

'You were out yourself at the time?'

'Yes. You know more about these things than I do, Mr
Maitland. Is it any good going back and having another
look myself?'

'At a guess I'd say not, but it can't do any harm. When the
police have gone through a place like that they've gone
through it thoroughly. I don't like the sound of this, Mr
Barrie, not one little bit. I suppose they've impounded the
rest of the knives in the set.'

'Yes, Mrs Hill was very indignant about that. They took
them away with them.'

'In that case it's child's play to trace the manufacturer,
find out exactly what the missing knife's measurements
are, and tell if it would fit the wounds. Where were those
knives kept, Mr Barrie, that it was so obvious immediately
that one was missing?'

'In a rack made to fit them, that was fixed to the wall just
over the chopping board.'

'And Mrs Hill, do you trust her?'

'She's looked after me ever since my wife died fifteen years ago. Perhaps,' said Owen, whose mind didn't seem to be altogether on the subject important though it was, 'if Nellie had lived David would have turned out differently.'

'Yes, perhaps.' It couldn't be denied that Maitland's agreement sounded a little perfunctory. 'We're talking about this woman though, Mrs Hill, I gather you're telling me you trust her.'

'Yes, of course, after all that time. As a matter of fact she's very indignant about all these enquiries the police are making.'

'That's only to be expected. However, you've talked to her, Mr Barrie. What time was it that she remembers seeing the knives last?'

'Four in the afternoon. She had everything ready for the oven then and washed the things she'd used while she was cooking. Then it's really quite reasonable that she didn't remember exactly putting it away, though I'm sure she would have put it in its usual place because she's just as much a creature of habit as the rest of us are.'

'And after that she didn't notice it again?'

'No.'

'You were home early yourself, Mr Barrie?'

'I told you that, and I explained why.'

'Yes, but this is important. Did you see Mrs Hill at that time?'

'No, not until after David had left. She came to ask me if he'd be in for dinner, and I had to tell her I'd be alone.'

'What do you know about her movements during that time?'

'She'd be in the kitchen, I imagine, or in the little sitting room we've made for her that leads off it. Except when she came through to set the table, but she'd be back and forth, nobody would have a chance to get in unseen.'

'Have you put that question to her specifically?'

'As a matter of fact, I have. She's quite sure nobody could have stolen the knife without her knowing.'

'That takes us to five past eight, am I right about that?' He sounded suddenly uncertain of himself.

'Yes, that's when she left. I was having my dinner.'

'How long did that occupy you, Mr Barrie?'

'Oh, I wouldn't say more than twenty minutes. It isn't much fun eating alone. Afterwards I was back and forth to the kitchen, and left the things I'd used stacked neatly by the sink. I'm afraid I'm a bit fussy about things like that.'

'And I suppose you didn't notice either whether the knife was in its proper place.'

Something rather sardonic in his tone seemed to worry Owen Barrie. He flushed a little and replied rather sharply, 'No, I didn't!'

'How long did this tidying operation of yours take?'

'Ten minutes, a quarter of an hour, I couldn't be certain.'

'Mr Barleycorn will have to see Mrs Hill of course —'

'If Owen is arrested,' said Desmond, 'she's certain to be called by the prosecution.'

'Yes, precisely. For that reason, my dear Desmond, I'd suggest you go home with Mr Barrie now and talk to her, before anyone can accuse us of tampering with the witnesses. But I was about to say, I don't suppose we'll get anything further from her. That leaves us with the period after, say, eight thirty-five until the time it was actually used during which it could have been extracted. Is there any way anyone could have got into the kitchen?'

'As a matter of fact . . . you're not going to believe this,' said Owen.

'Try me,' Maitland invited.

'Well, I don't carry a key to the back door, and neither did David as far as I know. But Mrs Hill told me there's a spare key, and as she's rather forgetful she keeps it hanging up in the porch.'

'Heaven and earth!' said Maitland. 'Where anybody in the world could get at it.'

'Well, yes. I told you you wouldn't believe me,' said Owen almost in a tone of satisfaction. 'She says nobody could see it, and showed me where it hung to prove it. But we don't bother about locking the outer door as well, and anyone had only to put his hand up, they wouldn't need to know it was there, it was such an obvious place.'

'I see. Well, I can imagine counsel for the prosecution having fun with that one,' said Maitland. 'Is there anything else you haven't told us, Mr Barrie?'

'I don't think so.'

'Let's hope you're right.'

'You think when they find the manufacturer, as you said, they'll prove it was the same knife?'

'In the ordinary way it shouldn't have gone missing in a well ordered household,' said Maitland. 'I'm very much afraid –' He broke off there, staring into space, but after a moment pulled himself together and changed the subject smoothly. 'When you said you wanted my help, Mr Barrie, I gather you had something else in mind than merely representing you in court.'

'You've a reputation for finding the truth in these kind of matters,' said Owen.

'My uncle has a less kind way of putting it. However, if I'm to help you you'll have to start by helping me. Can you think of anyone with a motive for encompassing these two deaths? I should explain that when an arrest is made it will be for one murder only, the one the prosecution think they can best prove. But I'm sure you'll agree that it wouldn't be reasonable to consider either of them separately.'

'Of course I realise that, but I can't think of anybody.'

'No friend or acquaintance they had in common who might conceivably have had a reason for wanting them both dead?'

'Only myself, Mr Maitland, only myself!'

'Well, all I can say is, don't repeat that to anyone but ourselves. And certainly if you get into court . . . but we'll talk
about that later when the worst happens. Meanwhile, if
you could think of any answer to my question I'd be glad if
you'd give it to me. At the moment I haven't an idea where
to begin.'

'Does that mean you don't believe me?'

'It means exactly what I said, Mr Barrie, no more, no less.
Now if you'll forgive me . . . Desmond is going to come
home with you – aren't you, Desmond? – to talk to Mrs Hill
while it's still possible for him to do so. Just don't forget, if
the police call on you again either with more questions or
with a warrant for your arrest, you're not saying anything.'
But he added to himself as he watched the two men leave
his room a few moments later, 'You've done quite enough
harm in that direction already.'

III

'Bit of a surprise,' said Vera that evening. As it was
Tuesday she and her husband were dining upstairs, and at
the moment they were all sitting over their sherry. It was a
warm evening, even for June, but the room was high
enough to catch what breeze there was, and the curtains
were billowing gently. 'Weren't you surprised, Nicholas?'
she demanded.

'I,' said Sir Nicholas, 'am never surprised. Though on this
occasion I must admit to having had a vague feeling that if
Antony was about to make a fool of himself it would be in
a different direction. Perhaps you will tell us exactly to
what you have committed yourself, my dear boy.'

Antony sipped his sherry before he replied. 'To undertaking Owen Barrie's defence if he's arrested,' he said

amiably. And then added, 'I like him, you know, and I'm sorry for him.'

'If you're trying to tell me he was justified in committing two murders –'

'Nothing of the sort, though come to think of it that's much what Desmond Barleycorn said when I asked him how he felt about undertaking the defence.'

'Well, this is one you shouldn't get into too deeply,' said his uncle.

'Why on earth not? It's quite an ordinary affair.'

'Nothing you take a hand in is ever ordinary,' said Sir Nicholas devastatingly. 'But if you want to know exactly what I meant I'll tell you. I've been thinking since we talked at lunch time –'

'No!'

'– and I think I've found the answer to Owen Barrie's rather odd action in calling upon Edward Coke to take on his defence.'

'It isn't exactly a mystery, Uncle Nick. The firm has been looking after his affairs since Edward Coke's father was alive, and in addition I gather he's feeling some remorse now for having misjudged the chap.'

'Well, that's one good thing that has come out of this,' said Jenny. 'Edward Coke has been vindicated.'

'If you're going to believe every word that's said to you –' Sir Nicholas began. Then he broke off. 'Still I agree with you, my dear, he wouldn't have told this story if it hadn't been true. It's far too incriminating.'

'That isn't why I believe it,' said Jenny.

'No, you believe it because it proves your husband was in the right all along. Very well, I'll apologise if it makes you feel any happier,' said Sir Nicholas, who never committed the crowning folly of defending the indefensible. 'I was taken in, fooled to the top of my bent.'

'But she was a very pretty woman,' said Antony, exchanging a grin with Vera.

'That, as you know perfectly well, had nothing whatever to do with it. But I was saying when you interrupted me, that I thought I could give you Barrie's reason for entrusting his defence to a firm with no criminal experience.'

'If you think there's something odd about it –'

'Of course it's odd,' snapped his uncle. 'You're not using your head, Antony. You've pointed out yourself that the two murders must be considered together. Very well then, if Barrie were innocent, who would be the only possible alternative suspect?'

'You mean Edward Coke don't you?'

'I hoped I had made myself sufficiently clear.'

'So Owen Barrie ... well, very properly of course, Edward wouldn't take the defence himself, but you're saying Barrie went to his firm in order to tie his hands.'

'Something like that. Now do you see,' said his uncle, 'why I say you shouldn't embroil yourself too deeply.'

Jenny began to look worried. 'But, Uncle Nick –'

'I'm just telling you, my dear, that if Antony starts meddling in this he may make some discoveries that he won't like at all. Either that his client is guilty, which should make his own position as defence counsel a difficult one –'

'You've told me often enough, Uncle Nick,' said Jenny firmly, 'it would only be his opinion. He wouldn't *know,* and wouldn't be entitled to act as if he did.'

'That's perfectly true,' said Sir Nicholas, with one of his sudden changes of mood. 'I'm not talking about his professional duty though, but his own peace of mind. On the other hand, if he discovers that Edward Coke is guilty ... what then? This young man, Desmond Barleycorn, is preparing the brief, but the name of the firm will be on it.

Are you telling me he's going to expose his own instructing solicitor in court?'

'Done it once,' said Vera. 'Told you all about that, Nicholas.'

Sir Nicholas shuddered. 'I can only be thankful it was a matter in which I was not involved. In any case the circumstances were different and the way it was done was different.' He turned to his nephew. 'Now do you see, Antony, why I'm asking you, pleading with you in fact, to treat this case just as any other. Do your best with the evidence in court and forget about the rest of it.'

'Yes, Uncle Nick,' said Antony, 'and I'm grateful for your views of course.'

'You don't agree with them.' Sir Nicholas's mood was rapidly changing again to the rather captious one he had displayed before. 'What's your solution then?'

'I haven't one, sir, but I do have a sort of idea,' Antony admitted.

'I've never known you yet when you didn't. I should be glad to hear it however.'

'I'm afraid it's too vague for that yet. I can tell you though, I don't really believe Owen Barrie did the murders. As far as that's concerned I think Elizabeth would have been more likely to murder him than the other way round, because he decided to tell the truth as David had admitted it to him.'

'Well, that's one way of looking at it,' said his uncle. 'An older man though, very much in love with a much younger woman and suddenly disillusioned about her feelings towards him. That's a pretty strong motive.'

'There's also David's murder.'

'But he was the one she'd betrayed him with. No, Antony, I don't think much of your reason for acquitting your client.'

'All right then, but just remember it's what I believe.

162

Let's go on to Edward Coke, then. I don't think he did it either.'

'I suppose you have some specious reason for that too.'

'Yes, indeed I do. If he'd been going to murder his wife and the man he must have suspected was her lover he'd have done it much earlier. You're going to tell me that's only an opinion too, Uncle Nick, and I admit it freely. But it's a feeling I have, and a very strong one.'

'You're going to neglect my advice then?'

'If Owen Barrie is arrested, yes.'

'But I don't see that a single line is open to you,' his uncle protested.

'I've encountered a few of the Barries' and the Cokes' friends in the course of the libel action. I'll start with them, perhaps they can tell me more. But not unless Sykes actually gets as far as making an arrest,' he added hastily, catching his uncle's eye. 'Unless my client is accused, I've no interest in the affair at all.'

His doubts were expelled almost before he had formulated them. Desmond Barleycorn telephoned later that evening, before Sir Nicholas and Vera had gone downstairs to their own quarters, to say that Owen Barrie was under arrest for the murder of Elizabeth Coke, and would come up before the magistrates the following morning. 'We shan't be putting on any defence so I can manage if you're busy,' he added, but Maitland, with an eye open for his uncle's reactions, reassured him smoothly:

'I'll be there.'

I

In general, where the case is a serious one, a Magistrates Court hearing is little more than a formality, to be followed speedily by the prisoner's committal for trial. To the defence, however, it has this advantage, that it is the first opportunity they have of assessing the main points of the prosecution's case. Not that it is necessary for all of these to be cited, merely enough to indicate that a trial is justified. Later of course the accused's solicitor will receive full details of the points that will be adduced against his client, but to Maitland at least the delay thus entailed could prove maddening.

This morning, however, the defence were in luck, if it could be regarded as fortunate that their worst suspicions were confirmed. A set of knives, the duplicate of the ones in the Barrie house, had been located – as Desmond had found from Mrs Hill when he talked to her the evening before, she had remembered quite well where they were bought – and the replica of the one that was missing was found to fit perfectly into the rather oddly shaped wounds Elizabeth Coke had received. After talking to the house-keeper the police, Maitland thought a little cynically, had had a busy day. It was likely that this had been the clinching fact when the decision was made to arrest Owen Barrie.

For the rest, the prosecution left motive strictly alone, except to say that a promise of marriage had existed between the accused and the deceased, and that Mr Barrie had admitted in a written statement that a serious disagreement had taken place between them immediately preceding Elizabeth Coke's death. The time and place of the killing, as well as the presumed murder weapon, told heavily against the prisoner. Maitland held his fire except for a not too strenuous protest when the prosecution wished to reserve what they called 'the not immediately pertinent' part of Barrie's statement until the trial, and the end was just as they expected. 'I can't help wishing the old boy had taken your advice,' said Desmond gloomily as they left the building, 'and pleaded guilty to manslaughter. I think when the whole story is told we could have got away with that nicely.'

'I think so too but you can't help admiring him for sticking to his guns like that. But I forgot, Desmond, you rather think he's guilty, don't you?'

'You see, I know Edward isn't,' said Desmond simply.

'And you still think he's the only alternative? I had all this out with my uncle last night and I can see another possibility.'

'Who?' That was Desmond at his most eager.

'I don't know who,' said Antony patiently. 'I just have the faintest glimmer of an idea about a possible motive. And I've no intention of making a fool of myself by explaining it to you at this stage, because I may very well be wrong.'

'I don't think that's fair at all,' Desmond grumbled. 'Anyway,' he added, much as Sir Nicholas had done, 'what are you going to do about it?'

'Well, I'm not going to crawl about on my hands and knees with a microscope looking for clues,' said Antony lightly, and was amused to see, as he had half expected, that Desmond's face fell. In some ways the solicitor was very young, younger than his years, 'I want to talk again to the people who gave evidence at the libel trial.'

'But they're only connected with the libel in the most – in the most tenuous way,' Desmond protested.

165

'That's very true, but they all belonged to the same set as the Cokes and the Barries if I may put it that way, something may emerge.'

'I should think it very unlikely,' said Desmond frankly.

'You're probably right, but I have to start somewhere. And clues in the storybook sense, Desmond, I'll leave to the police, who are quite capable of finding them for themselves. Though not always so capable of assessing them correctly,' he added, 'but that can't be helped. My concern is with people.'

'It sounds rather hit and miss,' said Desmond.

'More disillusionment!' Antony commented lightly. 'I'm really sorry to disappoint you, but that's the only way I can work. And I'd like another talk with Mary Jerrold too.'

Desmond came to a sudden full stop, to the great inconvenience to the people who were walking behind him. He turned an accusing look on Maitland. 'Unless you're lying to me, and you really do think Edward did it, I can't see what you should want with her again,' he said.

'I'm not lying to you,' said Antony evenly. He could understand and sympathise with Desmond's rather fierce defence of his friend and partner, and even admired him for it. 'If anyone can tell me anything about Elizabeth Coke it's Mary. I know she understood Coke's feeling about not being able to remarry even after a divorce, but in her own mind she must have looked on Elizabeth in some way as a rival. So I wouldn't mind betting she knew her through and through.'

'Oh, if that's all you want –' Desmond broke off there and grinned rather shamefacedly. 'When do you want to see all these people?' he asked resignedly.

'If it's convenient to you both, bring Miss Jerrold to Kempenfeldt Square tonight,' Antony suggested. 'I've an idea my uncle and aunt said they'd be out, so we can use the study. But I'm only asking you to be present at that interview, Desmond, to see fair play, in case you still don't trust me. I've got a feeling I might get more out of the others if I saw them alone.'

'But –'

'I know it isn't done. But I have a reputation for being unconventional, and I might as well make the most of it,' Antony told him. 'It isn't that I don't want your company,' he explained, 'it's just that I do feel people are much more likely to get confidential with only one other person present, than if there are two sitting waiting for their reply.'

'Yes, that makes sense. And to carry the idea to its logical conclusion ... does that mean you want to see the Walpoles and the Stowes separately?'

'That shouldn't be too difficult, should it? Walpole and Stowe will be at their places of business – I shouldn't say that about Terence Stowe, should I? He might be offended. But if I catch Walpole at his office and Stowe at the hospital, and see their wives at home –'

'It may be difficult to catch Joanna Stowe during the day. She's very taken up with this volunteer work she does.'

'Yes, so I gathered. And of course Mrs Walpole sometimes goes to the office with her husband. I'd forgotten that, this is going to be difficult.'

'Leave it to me to make the arrangements.' Desmond's buoyancy was returning. 'I know them, you see, so we can chat before I get down to making any definite appointment, and then I can suggest a time when I've gathered you'll be able to see them separately.'

'Thank you, that would be very helpful indeed. Will you take care of Miss Ross too?'

'Yes, there's no difficulty there, she's one of the idle rich. At least I'm not quite sure about the rich part, but idle at any rate.'

Antony glanced at his watch. 'If you come back to

167

chambers with me we can collect my uncle and all go to lunch together,' he suggested. 'He deplores my ways as much as you do – what's the quotation he uses? "Questioning is not the mode of conversation among gentlemen" – so you can sympathise with him over my unconventional ways. But don't unless you want to start a brawl in the restaurant, tell him that you won't be accompanying me on these proposed visits. He'd object to that and say so in no uncertain terms.'

'I can't believe that would make the slightest difference to you,' Desmond told him.

'Well no, of course not. But anything for a quiet life,' said Antony. 'Shall we walk or would you rather we looked for a cab?'

II

As it was still quite early Desmond elected to walk. They found Sir Nicholas in his room with his desk completely strewn with documents, and another pile at least a foot high on the floor beside him. He was glowering at the ones spread out in front of him in a rather distraught way, but pushed his spectacles on to his forehead as the two men went in, and after the introductions had been made expressed every willingness to leave his work immediately. They therefore made their way to Astroff's, where, as it was not yet one o'clock, Sir Nicholas's favourite table was waiting for them. The lunch passed off well except for one deliberate piece of provocation on Maitland's part. When his uncle fixed his instructing solicitor with a benevolent eye and said amiably, 'So you're the young man who's burdened with my nephew's assistance in this latest matter of his,' he interrupted Desmond's rather incoherent reply by saying:

168

'We don't altogether agree about our client, Uncle Nick. As I told you, I think he's innocent, but Desmond doesn't. He thinks he did it, but rather approves of his action. Justifiable homicide would just about sum it up.' Which led, as he had expected, to a brief homily on the sanctity of human life; but as this was addressed to him rather than to the youngest member of the party it didn't seriously impair Desmond's enjoyment of the occasion.

Afterwards they parted and uncle and nephew strolled back to the Inner Temple together. All would still have been well had not old Mr Mallory popped out of the clerks' room as soon as he heard the door. 'Good afternoon, Sir Nicholas,' he said. 'Mr Maitland, Chief Inspector Sykes is waiting for you. I took the liberty of having Willett show him to your room.'

'Thank you, Mallory,' said Antony, and just at that moment even this small politeness went very much against the grain. He knew perfectly well that Mallory was as aware as he was of Sir Nicholas's objection to some of his dealings with the police, and that he would much have preferred that the message be given privately. However, there was no help for it, he turned to meet his uncle's accusing look. 'He's the investigating officer in the Barrie case, Uncle Nick. He must want to talk to me about that.'

'So I suppose.' Sir Nicholas had reached his own door and spoke over his shoulder. 'However, I'm not so engrossed in this mass of papers that Collingwood had inflicted on me that I should not like to hear from you as soon as your visitor has gone.'

Antony said, 'Yes, of course,' as casually as he knew how, but truth to tell he was both puzzled and a little uneasy as to the cause of the visitation.

Chief Inspector Sykes was the only person Maitland knew who had ever succeeded in making himself look comfortable in one of the visitors' chairs in his office. 'I hope I didn't keep you waiting,' said Antony as he went in.

'My own fault, Mr Maitland, I should have called ahead. But when I'd had my lunch it was more or less on my way to drop in here so I thought I'd take a chance on seeing you. I did try to catch your eye in court this morning, but didn't succeed in doing so.'

'I saw you there too,' Antony admitted, 'while you were giving evidence. Afterwards you seemed to have disappeared.'

'So you've accepted a brief to defend Mr Owen Barrie on the charge of having murdered Elizabeth Coke,' said Sykes thoughtfully.

'I should have thought that was obvious. That can't be what you want to talk to me about, Chief Inspector. You know it isn't done.'

'Not about the case,' said Sykes carefully, 'but concerning it, if you see what I mean.'

'I don't I'm afraid.'

'You haven't forgotten, Mr Maitland, that it's barely eight weeks since you had Chief Superintendent Briggs in the witness box giving evidence for the defence in a murder trial.'

'Of course I haven't forgotten, but that was quite a different matter. I'm not thinking of calling him this time, if that's what you mean.'

'That's not what I mean and well you know it,' Sykes admonished him. 'I'm just trying to convey to you that he hasn't forgiven you for that, not by any means.'

'If that's a warning, Chief Inspector, I take it very kindly of you.' This was said in all sincerity; what Sykes had just said implied his complete trust in Antony's discretion, since Chief Superintendent Briggs was his immediate superior. 'There's nothing to worry about, you know. For that matter I don't suppose he ever will get over it, but it

170

won't make any difference to his attitude towards me. We've never got on.'

Sykes smiled in his sedate way at this understatement. 'I know he's always mistrusted you,' he said.

'As you have yourself on occasion, Chief Inspector.'

'I've thought once or twice that you weren't being completely open with us about things you knew,' said Sykes in his precise way. 'But this is rather different. I've every faith in your integrity.'

'And Briggs hasn't? That's a pity, but since I haven't stepped outside the law and don't intend to it can't really do me any harm.'

'I wouldn't be so sure about that, lad,' said Sykes seriously. 'What I'm trying to tell you is that this attitude of his is intensifying.'

'Even so –'

'He gets an idea into his head, you see,' said Sykes earnestly, 'and then nothing in the world will prove to him that he's wrong.'

'You ought to be talking to my uncle. He's told me that too.'

'Well, I wish I could make you believe it. This libel action for instance ... I take it you've no objection to my mentioning that to you, Mr Maitland.'

'It may be rather difficult to discuss that without imping-ing on the murder charge.'

'Precisely, but I think you ought to know what the Chief Superintendent thinks about your questioning of David Barrie.'

'I still don't understand.'

'He's saying that you provoked these murders by asking the young man whether he knew that Elizabeth Coke intended to marry his father.'

For a moment there was a silence. Maitland put up a hand to cover his eyes, and then let it drop again and

171

looked directly at his visitor. 'Don't you think I'm very conscious that that is probably true?' he asked.

'I'm sorry if I worded that badly. The point I wished to make was that Briggs thinks it was quite a deliberate action on your part. And to make it worse he thinks the question was completely without foundation.'

'Well, he's wrong about that. Owen Barrie had told me himself . . . and of course I never dreamed what the result would be.'

'Yes, Mr Maitland, but there's just one thing, and here I know I'm speaking out of turn but I hope we can trust each other by now.' He paused smiling. 'With the reservation I made a moment ago, of course.'

'Of course,' agreed Antony gravely.

'Then I may as well tell you that the prosecution's interpretation of Owen Barrie's statement will be that it's a complete lie, at least so far as Elizabeth Coke promising to marry him was concerned. If there's any argument about that your own statement during the libel action may come into question.'

'Let's leave that point for a moment. If they deny Barrie's statement they do away altogether with the motive, on which I should think they are relying pretty heavily.'

'They've got the opportunity and they've got the presumed murder weapon,' said Sykes. 'However, the court will be told that this engagement, or understanding, or whatever you like to call it was solely in Barrie's own mind, wishful thinking, you might say, and that when David came home and questioned him there was a furious quarrel – to which, as you know, he admits – and that that murder was committed out of jealousy.'

'He's not being tried for killing David.'

'I'm quite aware of that, Mr Maitland, but let me finish. The idea then is that Elizabeth Coke came round to see Owen Barrie out of pure consideration for his feelings,

172

thinking he must have misunderstood something she said, and wanting to put him straight about it. Jealousy again . . . do you see? That would explain the repeated stabbings, even though it was the first blow that killed her.'

'The first blow?' repeated Maitland sharply.

'Yes, as it happens.'

'That wasn't mentioned at the hearing.'

'No. If you remember –'

'Yes, the prosecution were playing their cards close to the chest. But what about David Barrie?'

'Certainly not the first blow that was struck. That's fairly easy to ascertain, you know. But at least three of his wounds might have proved fatal. But to get back to Elizabeth Coke, you do see how the theory fits the facts, don't you?'

'I'd be a fool if I didn't. The intention is obvious, of course, they're afraid we'll try for a lesser charge.'

'That, as I understand it, is the way the D.P.P. looks at it,' said Sykes. 'And I can't recall,' he added bitterly, 'ever having spoken so improperly to a defence counsel before. But it's your position that concerns me. Could we go back to that?'

'If you like. I imagine you're concerned with what would happen if Owen Barrie is found guilty.'

'That's it exactly. It could be said you introduced this matter into the libel action without any foundation in fact, and that that part of Barrie's statement which the prosecution claims to be untrue was made at your instigation.'

'At least it's better than being charged with nobbling the witnesses,' said Maitland with an attempt at lightness. 'That was it last time, wasn't it?'

'It's no laughing matter,' Sykes reproved him. 'It would still be subornation of perjury, that is, if Barrie repeats the substance of his statement in court, and it wouldn't be a very nice story to get about.'

'No, I'm quite aware of that. And if I do manage to find a witness or witnesses to confirm my own ideas –'

'There's no knowing what might happen,' said Sykes definitely.

'But surely –' He broke off as a thought struck him. 'Look here, Sykes, are you telling me Briggs is going off his rocker?'

'Certainly not, Mr Maitland.' Sykes's cautious soul was shaken to the core. 'But I won't deny, he added reluctantly, 'that on this one subject alone –'

'You mean I've become a sort of obsession with him? Well, all I can tell you, Chief Inspector, is that I intend to stick firmly to the paths of righteousness, that should take care of everything, shouldn't it?'

'I'm not talking about proof of any wrongdoing, Mr Maitland, only about gossip, about what might be said.' He came to his feet as he spoke. 'I haven't asked about Mrs Maitland's health,' he said, 'or about Lady Harding and your uncle either.'

Antony smiled at him. 'No, and that's the first time I remember your ever starting a conversation in any other way,' he said. 'They're all well, thank you, and I'm grateful too for the warning. I needn't tell you that the rest of our conversation remains strictly between the two of us.'

'Sir Nicholas will certainly ask you –'

'Yes, I know. I'll have to tell him you warned me to look out for Briggs, but it needn't go any further than that. And if Mallory hadn't greeted us when we came in from lunch with the information that you were here,' he added, 'I shouldn't mention your visit at all. He's got a bit of a bee in his bonnet himself about the subject, and this will only confirm his worst fears.'

However, there was no use making things worse than they were already. Maitland went straight to his uncle's room when he had seen Sykes out and watched for a

174

moment as the detective stumped down the rather dark staircase. 'Well?' said Sir Nicholas as he went in.

'He's as bad as you are, Uncle Nick. A sort of gypsy's warning about Chief Superintendent Briggs.'

Sir Nicholas frowned. 'I fail to see on what he could base any insinuations against you in this matter,' he said.

'Well, so do I.' He sustained a rather hard look from his uncle, and went on in a hurry, 'The thing is, you see, I think after all these years Sykes has developed a liking for me. He's seeing trouble where none exists.'

'I suppose,' said Sir Nicholas coldly, 'that what you're trying to tell me – or rather not to tell me – is that you very improperly discussed every aspect of the case with him. Well,' he added after a moment when Antony was silent, 'I won't press you about that, but I should like you to bear in mind that both Vera and I have said very much the same thing to you in the past about Superintendent Briggs, though with rather more basis, we both feel, than the gypsy's warning you spoke of so glibly a moment ago.'

'I'm tired of saying that I don't intend to do anything that could possibly cause trouble.'

Sir Nicholas's changes of mood were sometimes bewildering. At this point he underwent one such reversal and smiled at his nephew almost benignly. 'There's no point in arguing the matter is there? May I borrow one of your own phrases, Antony, and say who lives may learn?'

III

It was Maitland's practice, and had been ever since the start of his professional life, to borrow Sir Nicholas's study when the occasion arose for him to conduct an interview at home, provided of course that its owner was otherwise engaged. He had confirmed that evening that his uncle and

Vera would be dining out, and that they had no objection to his temporary occupation of their favourite room. He had arranged with Desmond to bring Mary Jerrold round after dinner, and for once in his life the young man's eagerness didn't get them there too early. Or perhaps it was Mary's influence that had restrained him. In any case, it was just after nine o'clock when Gibbs announced on the house phone that there were two visitors for Mr Maitland. Until Vera had joined the household he had always refused in his cross-grained way to use the instrument that had been installed for his convenience, but had insisted on making everybody feel guilty by tramping upstairs with messages. Now Antony was grinning as he put down the phone and turned to look at Jenny. 'I'm always expecting Gibbs to regress into the ways he had before Uncle Nick married Vera,' he said, 'but I think we're fairly safe now, don't you? He's showed no sign of it.'

'She might even persuade him to retire some day,' said Jenny hopefully. But her husband shook his head at that, he'd long since given up hope.

Mary Jerrold and Desmond Barleycorn were awaiting him in the study. His first thought was that Mary was ill at ease, his second that perhaps in the circumstances that wasn't surprising. He did his best to get her settled comfortably, and to relax the atmosphere by means of a little general conversation before he started his question-ing, going so far as to seat himself on the sofa where he could view both his visitors with equal ease, though being in a rather uncertain mood himself he would much have preferred to be wandering around the room. But his good–natured intention was to some extent frustrated by Mary Jerrold, who was sitting straight-backed on the very edge of Sir Nicholas's comfortable chair, and interrupted a remark of his about the warm spell they were enjoying by saying abruptly, 'I can't think why you wanted to see me again.'

'I thought perhaps Desmond might have explained it to you,' said Antony. Desmond gave him a reproachful look, being as much in the dark as the girl was. He hadn't believed Maitland's rather specious explanation, and he didn't believe it now, hearing it for the second time. 'You see, Miss Jerrold,' Antony went on, 'in any murder investigation it's of vital importance to know something about the character of the victim. In your particular circumstances I thought perhaps you might be able to tell me more than anybody else about Elizabeth Coke.'

'Except Edward,' said Mary after she had considered this remark for a moment. 'He ought to know her better than anybody else.'

'I don't agree with you there. In the beginning he was in love with her, and they say love is blind, don't they? And after that . . . I think he would be inclined to put his own interpretation on her actions, because they concerned him so nearly.'

'Well, I'll do my best, of course, but I don't know anything at all about David Barrie.'

'You had met him however.'

'Yes, I told you that, didn't I? I thought him rather affected, rather negligible as a person,' said Mary. 'And I liked Owen Barrie very much, only he was as blind as anybody else to Elizabeth's faults. You're quite right about that, Mr Maitland, I sometimes thought I was the only person who saw through her and I'd be very glad if you could do something for Mr Barrie even though I've got a feeling that Desmond thinks he really did both the murders. Only not at Edward's expense of course . . . clearing Owen Barrie, I mean.'

'I'm sure Desmond explained that to you at least, it's the last thing in my mind.'

That brought the relaxation that he'd been striving for so unsuccessfully before. She smiled at him warmly and said,

'Then I'll do all I can to help you. What do you want to know?'

'It's difficult to put it to you without asking you leading questions,' said Maitland. Sitting there in a dress of some silky material in a soft blue she looked about as little like a lawyer as anything he could have imagined, and he had to stop himself on the point of explaining that remark. 'Perhaps if I tell you what Edward said about his wife you could tell me if you agree with it.'

'Edward wouldn't lie to you.'

'My dear Miss Jerrold, you mustn't take me up so quickly. I'm not insinuating anything of the kind. Only, as I explained to you, I think his opinion may be coloured by their relationship.'

'I'm sorry,' she said contritely. 'What did Edward tell you about Elizabeth?'

'That she was frigid,' said Antony simply. And wondered as he spoke whether the day would ever come when Edward Coke and this girl who was so much in love with him would be completely open with each other and the whole story of his disastrous marriage would be told.

The result of his remark was to bring Mary upright again. 'But that's nonsense,' she said. 'She was – I can't think of any way to put it except vulgarly, Mr Maitland – she was one of the sexiest women I've ever known.'

'Was she though?'

'But surely Edward –'

'I don't think I can go into his reasons for being mistaken, Miss Jerrold, though I think I understand them. Will you tell me your reasons for your opinion?'

'You're thinking I'm prejudiced,' she said accusingly.

'It's exactly because I don't think that I wanted to talk to you again,' he told her, and now for the first time Desmond began to believe him. 'I think your training in the law has probably taught you to weigh evidence very shrewdly, though I don't know you very well, of course, so I may be wrong. But be a good girl and tell me –'

'You know I used to dine with them fairly regularly, usually when Desmond was there too. And generally there'd be one or two other couples, and it was very noticeable – I'm afraid you won't regard this as proof, Mr Maitland – that she'd make a dead set at every one of the men present, and not one of them could resist her. I should think she could twist any man alive round her little finger. I wonder Desmond didn't tell you that.'

'I never noticed,' said Desmond simply. 'And if you want to know why,' he added suddenly under heaven knows what compulsion, 'it's because I had eyes only for you, old girl.'

Mary stared at him for a moment. 'Oh Desmond!' she said, obviously torn between remorse and exasperation, 'I thought . . . and all this time I've been telling you about my feelings for Edward. I didn't mean to hurt you.'

'You didn't,' said Desmond, though whether that was true or not Antony couldn't decide. 'And if you want to know how I feel about Elizabeth's death,' he added defiantly, 'I'm glad Edward's free. You'd never have changed your mind as long as he considered himself tied to her, but this way it's a straight match between us. And if you think,' he added, turning rather fiercely to Maitland, 'that gives me a motive for killing her you're quite right. Only it so happens I didn't.'

'Motives seem to be building up thick and fast,' said Maitland mildly. 'Yours is one I haven't considered, as a matter of fact.' As he spoke he allowed his eyes to move back to the girl, and Desmond spoke again almost as though he had made an open accusation.

'If you're thinking that Mary –'

'The thought had crossed my mind,' Antony admitted. So far as he knew he'd got all he was going to get out of the

179

conversation, and was interested to see where this particular line might lead.

'Let me remind you then that David Barrie was killed too,' Desmond snapped. 'You can't say she had a motive for that.'

'I can think of one,' said Mary. She sounded almost amused, certainly not offended by Maitland's frankness.

'Can you though? Expound,' Antony invited.

'The libel action had tied David and Elizabeth together in everyone's minds, so that when they were both killed the same evening it would seem obvious that it was something to do with that. David's death would hide the real motive.' She paused a moment and then laughed outright. 'I'm sorry, Desmond, that applies to you too.'

'Perhaps it does, but no-one would think such a thing of you,' said Desmond huffily. 'You couldn't possibly be so – so devious.'

'It might be said it would take a woman to think of a thing like that,' Mary pointed out. 'Though as a matter of fact,' she added more seriously, 'I don't think I could stick a knife into anybody. I don't think I could bring myself to do it.'

'No, I don't think so either,' Maitland agreed. 'But I just wish everyone was as frank as you, Miss Jerrold. Now you've told me that the Barries were sometimes asked to dine with the Cokes at the same time as you, and Elizabeth flirted with both of them. And told each of them afterwards, I suppose,' he added thoughtfully, 'that she did it because she didn't want their relationship to become obvious.'

'Yes, I'm sure that's how it was. I don't think I've explained very well. Her behaviour varied with every man she came into contact with. Owen Barrie for instance, I think he's rather an old-fashioned person, and I'm sure he thought she was as pure as the driven snow.'

'Yes, I see, it's a very good point. Who else did you meet at the Cokes' dinner table?'

'Primrose Ross sometimes, and the Walpoles and the Stowes. There was another couple once or twice – different ones I mean – but those were just casual meetings and I don't even remember their names.'

'Can you, Desmond?'

'I'm afraid not. The people Mary's mentioned were their particular friends.'

'All right then, Miss Jerrold, did she play the same game with Mr Walpole and Mr Stowe?'

'Oh, yes.'

'Did they respond?'

'Each in his own way. Roland Walpole indulging her rather good-naturedly I thought, rather as though he were dealing with a child; and Terence Stowe rather more cautiously. I suppose in the medical profession one has to be especially careful.'

Antony smiled at her. He was finding this interview unexpectedly enjoyable. 'You know, Miss Jerrold, that's the nearest you've come to a catty remark,' he said.

'Except about Elizabeth, of course,' said Mary seriously.

'Yes, except for that. You've been very frank with me and I'm truly grateful for that. And to you, Desmond, of course.' They talked for a little longer but nothing else emerged, so he saw them on their way – Gibbs had already retired for the night, it being past ten o'clock – and went upstairs to regale Jenny with an account of what had passed.

'But I don't understand,' said Jenny, 'any more than Mary Jerrold did, why Edward Coke was so deceived in his wife. I can quite see why you didn't explain it to her of course, but I'm different, you're always indiscreet with me.'

'Only because you're the soul of discretion yourself, love. I wonder sometimes ... doesn't all this legal shop bore you? If anything it's got worse since Vera married Uncle Nick.'

'You know it doesn't. In fact I sometimes think I know as much about it as you do,' said Jenny.

'Except, my dearest love, that you haven't a logical mind,' Antony pointed out, laughing at her. 'And thank heaven for that,' he added. 'If you were to start being reasonable –'

Jenny laughed back at him, but wasn't to be diverted from her point. 'You were going to tell me –' she said insinuatingly.

'Oh yes, about Edward Coke. Well, to begin with he fell head over heels in love with Elizabeth, and he must have been in his middle thirties at the time, let me remind you.'

'Like the man in the song,' said Jenny.

'What song?' Antony's mind was on what he was saying, and for a moment she had him puzzled.

'When he thinks that he is past love, it is then he meets his last love,' said Jenny, thinking quite rightly that this was explanation enough.

'Oh, I see. But I don't think Edward Coke was quite like that,' Antony told her. 'I can't imagine him ever – what was it? – flirting gaily with two or three or more. He was quite determined that when he married it would be for good, and perhaps he isn't a very susceptible man himself, I wouldn't know about that, or perhaps he picked on thirty-five, say, as being a time at which he might be expected to know his own mind. Anyway, he was in love with her, and naturally all he saw was perfection. And their marriage seems to have been perfectly normal for a few months, then she started to withdraw from a close relationship, and eventually elected to have a separate bedroom. I think, as you know, that she married him for his money, or rather for the expected legacy from Aunt Harriet, so it might well be that she developed a distaste for his lovemaking. But he wouldn't want to see it that way, what man would? I expect he rationalised it – I hate jargon, but it's the only word I can think of – by telling himself that she was naturally cold

182

with everybody, and once he'd done that he shut his eyes firmly to her attitude to other men, or perhaps thought it mere playfulness.'

'Yes, that's perfectly reasonable,' said Jenny. 'Antony, wouldn't it be awful –'

'Yes, it would, but as it isn't we needn't worry about it,' said Antony firmly. 'I think after all that we deserve some of the cognac we keep for Uncle Nick, don't you? All this plain speaking takes it out of one.'

'Yes, I like the sound of Mary Jerrold,' said Jenny, answering the spirit rather than the letter of what he said. She was rummaging in the cupboard, but as the Hardings had been with them only yesterday evening the bottle wasn't far to seek. 'What I do wonder,' she added, straightening herself, 'is which of the two she'll choose in the end. Edward Coke, or your friend Desmond.'

'I don't know and just at the moment I don't care,' said Antony accepting his glass. 'Anyway, I don't know if Desmond still regards me as a friend after my bluntness this evening.'

'Oh, I'm sure he does, or he wouldn't have practically proposed marriage in front of you.'

'Is that how you see it?'

'Yes, of course.'

'You may be right. However, what concerns me is Owen Barrie's coming trial, and how the devil I'm to get him out of the mess he's in.'

It wasn't until later when they were both in bed that he remembered Sykes's visit and the warning words he had uttered. He hadn't mentioned either to Jenny, and didn't intend to, but neither would Uncle Nick so that was all right. All the same it seemed to be unusually hard to get to sleep.

I

In spite of Antony's misgivings Desmond sounded perfectly friendly when he called on Friday morning. 'Sorry to have been so long about it,' he started.

'It didn't seem long,' said Antony truthfully. The contract seemed more complicated than ever, and the days not long enough to unravel its intricacies. 'Are you going to tell me you've arranged some appointments for me?'

'That's right. For today, if that isn't too short notice.'

'Not a bit of it. I said, if you remember, I'd prefer to make it soon. Mallory tells me I shall probably be in court all next week.'

'That's good then. I did a bit of sleuthing of my own, and found out when you could get hold of Roland and Frances, and Terence and Joanna separately.'

'That's good.'

'Frances will be at the office today, but I was rather cunning there,' said Desmond, obviously pleased with himself. 'I said you wanted to see Roland, and made an appointment with him for ten-thirty. He said he couldn't give you more than half an hour because he had to leave then to see a client. I thought you could hang about and talk to Frances after he'd gone.'

'That sounds perfectly feasible. Well done!'

'As for Terence and Joanna, it was a bit more tricky. He's operating this morning and I think anyway he's not too keen on having you turn up at the hospital.'

'Yes, it might be misconstrued,' Antony agreed.

'However, he said he'd be through by lunchtime, and

would go home and see you there. I don't think he's too pleased about it though, he said it would mean his working late. And that's where your talk with Joanna comes in. She gets home about four o'clock and I gather Terence will be at least two hours after that. So if you could see her at that time —'

'Better and better. That only leaves Primrose Ross.'

'I didn't make an appointment with her, I wasn't quite sure how long these various interviews of yours would take. But it shouldn't be difficult to get hold of her just when it suits you. If you miss her the first time you could try again.'

'Yes, of course, I'll do that.'

'And you're sure you don't want me to come with you?'

'Quite sure, Desmond. It's only this question of thinking they may talk more easily when we're alone,' he explained again. 'Did you and Miss Jerrold get home safely last night?'

'I think what had been said has made a certain stiffness between us,' Desmond admitted, but he didn't sound too cast down. 'I suppose you think it was stupid of me sounding off like that, but it always seemed so hopeless before.'

'I don't quite follow your reasoning there, I'm afraid.'

'Oh, the unattainable is always so much more attractive,' said Desmond. 'Anyway, Mary was pretty thoughtful, I'd call that a good sign myself, wouldn't you?'

'I don't know whether I'm a very good judge of such things, but I think you may be right.'

'That's good. And you will let me know what happens,' he added anxiously.

'Well, naturally. Don't count on anything though, Desmond. It's a counsel of despair really.' And that, he thought as he hung up the receiver, just about sums it up.

However there was this much consolation to be had, he could leave the now hated contract behind him. Roland

Walpole received him amiably and showed no surprise at seeing him alone. 'Quite understandable,' he said, when Antony attempted an explanation. 'Sometimes it's embarrassing having the womenfolk around.'

'That's it exactly,' said Maitland with relief. 'There are two things I want to consult you about, Mr Walpole, and quite frankly I'm only doing so as a last resort.'

'You're very welcome to anything I can tell you, but I can't for the life of me think how I can be of help.'

'One thing is that I'd like to know what you thought of Elizabeth Coke.' 'That,' he added smiling, 'is where I thought you might be more frank with me if Mrs Walpole wasn't present.'

'And how right you were. Not that I thought anything of it until I saw that letter from Primrose, just assumed it was Elizabeth's way.'

'What exactly –?'

'Sending out signals to every man she met. Most embarrassing, as a matter of fact, when Edward was there, not to mention Fran, of course, but luckily she's an understanding sort of person. And frankly I thought, as I said, it was just Elizabeth's way, and didn't mean anything in particular.'

'She didn't,' Antony hazarded, 'strike a responsive cord in you?'

'I'm human,' said Roland, 'she was a very pretty if not a beautiful woman. But I'm happily married, to put it bluntly Fran is a darling, so though I must admit to being flattered I never thought to carry things any further.'

'Do you think Mrs Coke would have agreed if you had made such a proposal?'

'That's something we'll never know.'

'You say that until you saw the libellous letter you thought it was just her way.'

'I gave her the benefit of the doubt, I suppose. After all Edward is an old friend, and as his wife she deserved my

186

consideration. But when I saw what she was saying I didn't hesitate a moment between them. I gather David Barrie admitted in court that there was something between him and Elizabeth after all, but I wish you could prove the whole thing was a lie.'

'I think I may say we're in a fair way to doing so.' Roland looked interested, but Antony stopped there firmly. Mainly because to go any further would have been an unjustifiable indiscretion, but also because he wondered suddenly whether what he was saying was true in view of Sykes's revelations the day before.

'Yes, I suppose it's none of my business,' said Roland cheerfully. 'I wonder if Edward will marry that little Jerrold girl now.'

'Has he ever spoke to you about her?'

Roland's eyes narrowed. 'I didn't think you were here to talk about Edward,' he said. 'And, no, he's a cautious old stick, and has never said a word about it. But I've seen them together, and her feeling for him was perfectly obvious.'

'I see. To go back to Elizabeth Coke, leaving Mr Coke aside for the moment, do you know anything about her relationships with other men?'

'Only with Owen Barrie, and from what he told me with David,' said Roland. 'As far as anyone else was concerned, they may have been as uninterested as I was. And I wouldn't be telling you about Owen, if I weren't damn sure you knew exactly what he told me already. He phoned me that night, the Thursday, the night that Elizabeth and David were killed.'

Maitland, who had been lounging in his chair, now sat up very straight indeed. 'That,' he said, 'is something that my client did not choose to confide in me.' He was fumbling as he spoke for one of the tattered envelopes on which he was accustomed to make notes, usually illegible ones.

187

'As a greater man than I said, your story interests me strangely.'

'Well, he may not have told you that he'd told me,' said Roland, 'which is a bit complicated but I don't know how else to put it. But I'm quite sure he told you the same things. He's a very intelligent man, you know, and I imagine he realises his only hope is to get away with a plea of manslaughter.'

Perhaps that was something better not commented upon for the moment. 'Go on, Mr Walpole,' said Antony in an expressionless tone.

'He said David had come home from the court very upset, and demanding to know whether it was true that there was something between his father and Elizabeth. Owen told him then that as soon as she was free they would announce their engagement, and in the course of their subsequent conversation David, in great distress, admitted to his father that the whole story about Edward was a lie from beginning to end, and that Elizabeth had promised to marry him too, which was why he'd agreed to back her up.'

'At what time did this conversation take place?'

'I didn't notice exactly, though when we talked about it the next morning Fran said it was almost exactly nine o'clock.'

'Had you had any idea before that that there was anything between her and either of the Barries?'

'Not really. Certainly, I'm sure Owen never embarked on an affair with her, that wouldn't be his style at all. As for David, I thought he was too much of a lightweight, that she wouldn't really be interested in him. And perhaps that's the truth of the matter after all.'

'Do I gather from what you say, Mr Walpole, that you believe Owen Barrie to be guilty?'

'In the strict sense I suppose the answer to that is, yes.

But I think he must have been so upset by the disclosures that he didn't know what he was doing. I don't know what's best to do of course, that's your department. Either manslaughter, as I said, or temporary insanity, I suppose.'

'Did you read the account of the Magistrates' Court hearing?'

'Yes, I did.'

'Then you may have noticed that Mr Barrie pleaded not guilty.'

'But surely you told him –'

'I couldn't tell him how to plead, Mr Walpole, but I pointed out the advantages – the possible advantages – of pleading guilty to a lesser charge. He's quite adamant however, that he didn't do it.'

'What I don't understand ... it isn't that I want to think him guilty, I'm sure you know that, Mr Maitland, but I don't see who else could have had a motive.'

'No, that is a problem.'

'If it had been just David or just Elizabeth –'

'Exactly, but it was both of them. The other way I thought you might help me, Mr Walpole, is in the way of giving evidence as to character. I gather you have a high opinion of Owen Barrie.'

'The highest. And of course I'd be very happy to do what I can, but suppose the prosecution ask me what I think really happened?'

'I should object to their questioning you on a matter of opinion, as you aren't an expert witness, and I'm pretty sure the judge would uphold me.' He glanced at his watch. 'As a matter of fact, it's just occurred to me that perhaps Mrs Walpole might be able to help me in this way too. I know you have an appointment, but if I could have a word with her before I leave –'

'Why yes, of course, that's a very good idea. But I think you'll find her opinion very much like mine, though perhaps she's even more vehemently in Owen's favour.' He got up as he spoke and began to shuffle papers together in an absent-minded way that convinced Maitland his mind was very far away from what he was doing. 'If you'll forgive me then,' he said. 'I'll ask Fran to join you in here, shall I? And I'll tell my secretary you're not to be disturbed.'

Antony thanked him and watched him go. When Fran Walpole came in he had wandered to the window and was looking down at the traffic in the narrow street below. This office was in one of the more modern buildings, but the furniture had obviously come from a former place of business, giving it an air of comfort that he enjoyed.

Fran Walpole surprised him by giving him both her hands in greeting as though he was an old friend. 'I thought I was to be excluded from the conference,' she said.

'I just wanted to see you both separately, Mrs Walpole. Sometimes that makes people feel less – less constrained in what they say.'

She smiled at that. 'You wanted to ask Roland what he thought of Elizabeth Coke without my inhibiting presence,' she asserted. 'She was pretty much of a man-eater, you know, and would have made a meal of him if he'd let her. But I don't think she ever got a chance.'

'Last time I talked to you you said –'

'Elizabeth was alive then,' said Frances as though that made all the difference, which perhaps it did.

'You used the word, demure.'

'Well, so she was, on the surface, when she wished to be.'

'But underneath –'

'I'm quite willing to be open with you, Mr Maitland, if knowing the truth will help you help Owen. But all I can give you is opinion, not proof, which I suppose is why I wasn't franker with you before. Let's sit down over here and be comfortable, Mr Maitland, I'm not particularly busy

190

and can give you all the time you want.'

'I don't think what I have to ask you will take very long.'

'I dare say not, but there is also what I want to ask you,' she said. 'Did Roland tell you that Elizabeth was pretty much of a bitch?'

'He didn't put it quite like that. And I think he thought her ways were pretty harmless until you showed him the letter. And even then I don't think he quite believed it until Owen Barrie telephoned him the night she died.'

'That's men all over, never can see what's under their noses,' Fran grumbled. 'I'd no reason to be jealous, Mr Maitland, so I think my opinion is probably as good a one as you'll get. If you want me to tell the court that what happened was more her own fault than anybody else's I'll be glad to.'

'I'm afraid it isn't quite as easy as that, Mrs Walpole.'

'But Roland said –'

'Yes, he gave me his opinion too. But Mr Barrie is pleading not guilty,' Antony told her.

'I read that in the paper, but I thought it just meant not guilty by reason of insanity, or temporary insanity, or something like that. I don't understand these things, but it seems quite obvious to me.'

'Yes, I'm afraid –' He broke off there, staring at her.

'Afraid of what, Mr Maitland?' she prompted him after a moment.

'Afraid that's what everyone will think.'

'But isn't that the best way out?'

'Not if he didn't do it.'

'But you can't separate one murder from the other, and nobody else had a motive for both. Please don't misunderstand me, I'm fond of Owen, I think the situation is a perfectly horrible one, but I don't see how we can any of us get out of it without his being hurt.'

'Well, one of the things I came to ask you was your

191

opinion of Elizabeth Coke, and you've given me that in no uncertain terms. The other was to ask you if you'd be willing to give character evidence on Mr Barrie's behalf, and that's the reason I gave your husband for saying I wanted to see you as a matter of fact, as though it was an afterthought. And if you still believe Mr Barrie's guilty and are afraid the prosecution may ask you awkward questions, I'll tell you right away what I told Mr Walpole . . . I shouldn't let them.'

'I shouldn't care,' Fran asserted.

'I meant awkward to the defence, Mrs Walpole, not awkward to you. I'm sure you'd be quite equal to taking on the most terrifying of prosecuting counsel.'

'I don't know about that, but I do know I'd like to help Owen,' she said. 'And at least when he's tried all this horrible business about Edward will be cleared up. And that's one thing to be thankful for.'

No good pointing out to her the possible difficulties, but Barrie's telephone call to her husband might have been carefully thought out in preparation for what was to come. 'Mrs Walpole, you used the term man-eater a moment or two ago. We know now that she had her claws into Owen Barrie, if I may put it that way –'

'Yes, but that's where she was so clever. Owen is an old-fashioned man you know, with an old-fashioned sense of what's right. She attracted him by playing the misunderstood martyr, someone too good for this wicked world in fact.'

'Yes, that seems in character. There was also David Barrie. Somebody said she regarded him as negligible.'

'Another woman,' said Fran wisely. 'I dare say she did, but you'll never tell me she persuaded him to tell those lies for her without sleeping with him.'

'No, I see what you mean. Now the question is, as you told me you're probably my best source of information, can you think of anybody else who was under her spell?'

That brought a frown and a silence long enough to become uncomfortable. 'I don't like to talk about my friends,' she said at last, and then smiled at him in a rather deprecating way. 'What else have I been doing ever since you came in?' she asked rhetorically. 'But that's only because I want to help Owen. But I really do think he was responsible, you know, so I don't see why I should start a wild goose chase about somebody else.'

'Then I must apologise for taking up so much of your time,' said Antony, getting to his feet. She was beside him in an instant, a hand on his arm.

'Have I disappointed you very much, Mr Maitland?' she asked. 'I'm truly sorry about that.'

He could have said, I think you've given me exactly what I wanted, but he was pretty sure by now that that would only frighten her. Besides, there was the uncomfortable point that having the information he needed didn't mean he knew how to make use of it. 'Try not to worry, Mrs Walpole,' he said. And then on an impulse, 'One of the consolations of this rather sordid job of mine is that it sometimes brings me into contact with people like you and your husband.'

She was smiling again when he left, but he wondered how much reassurance his words had really given her.

II

Terence Stowe would be at home about lunch time, Desmond had said, and that was vague enough. But luck was with him, when he arrived he found that his quarry was there before him.

Terence Stowe seemed more relaxed today. He offered his visitor a drink, but confined himself to black coffee in which Antony joined him. 'I gather you feel Edward is completely vindicated now,' Stowe said. 'I hope you haven't come to tell me I ought to apologise for thinking the worst of him.'

'No, nothing like that. I'm concerned now with Mr Barrie's defence. But did Owen Barrie telephone you too? There were no details in the paper.'

'Weren't there? I didn't notice. I was in court on Thursday afternoon, a week ago that is – and may I say I admired your performance very much.'

'Oh, I see. I thought you'd been excused from further attendance because of your professional duties. Anyway, I think you're right, we can leave Edward Coke's affairs to take care of themselves from now on. As I said –'

'Yes, I heard you. A pretty thankless task I should have thought, not that I don't wish you the best of luck.'

'I'd be grateful if you'd tell me your view of the matter, Mr Stowe.'

'Why, the obvious one I should have thought. It's possible nowadays to get off more lightly if the provocation has been very great. Isn't that right?'

'Yes, it is. But Mr Barrie's plea is not guilty, plain and unadorned.'

'You mean there'll be no mention of extenuating circumstances?'

'Precisely,' said Antony, and heard in his own voice an echo of his uncle's tone.

'Well, that's a turn up for the books,' said Terence. 'And you want to talk to me about it? What on earth can I do for you?'

'You know the Barries well?'

'Certainly I do, and have a great regard for Owen.'

'Then if we decide to use evidence of good character –?'

'That's a last resort, isn't it? Anyway I'd be very glad to co-operate, but all I could say would be that he wouldn't have done such a thing in his right mind.'

'In that case we'd better take you off the list, hadn't we? There is one other thing you might help us with though. You may know that the defence in a case of this kind is often as concerned with the character of the victim as with that of the accused.'

'That seems reasonable. Now David, I should have said, is a natural murderer, a light-hearted chap without any sense of morals at all. He was bound to get into trouble sooner or later.'

'That's interesting, of course, but I'm really more concerned with Elizabeth Coke.'

'Yes, I suppose you would be,' said Terence slowly. 'Owen is only accused of her murder, isn't he?'

'That's the custom.'

'And I suppose in that case they take the killing that's more easily proved,' said Terence thoughtfully. 'Well that shouldn't be difficult. If Owen took her seriously –'

'You don't think she was serious about marrying him then?' Antony enquired.

'Oh, I shouldn't think so.'

'Not even for his money?'

'Well ... perhaps.' He seemed to make the admission reluctantly. 'My own impression was that she was more interested in having a good time.'

'Yes, I've been learning this and that about Mrs Coke ever since she was murdered,' said Antony. 'Surprising what a difference that has made to people's willingness to talk.'

'Can you wonder? And I did tell you the truth when you saw me before – when you saw Joanna and me together – we both believed Elizabeth's story. But I certainly wouldn't have wanted to admit with my wife present that she was ... well ... a sensual woman.'

'That knowledge might provide us with an alternative suspect,' Maitland told him.

'I think it very unlikely. I don't know anyone who would have been fool enough to take her seriously, except Owen I'm afraid.'

'You seem to know a great deal about her, Mr Stowe.'

'Not more than anybody else.'

Maitland ignored that. 'Would you say that was because you had a fling with her yourself at one time?' he asked.

Terence looked at him blankly for a moment. 'Strictly between you and me, and you needn't think you'll get me into court to give evidence to this effect, we did have a brief affair. But it was over some time ago with no hard feelings on either side.'

'I see. Didn't that make you a little more disinclined to believe her story about her husband's activities?'

'Not a bit. I don't think one thing had anything to do with the other. Of course I know now I was wrong about Edward, but I don't see how you could have expected me to have guessed that at the time he brought the libel action.'

'No, I suppose not. Well,' he went on, coming to his feet, 'I'm grateful for your time Mr Stowe and only sorry you can't help me. I'd better leave you to get your lunch now.'

'As a matter of fact I'm going straight back to the hospital, I'll get something in the canteen there. I only came home because Desmond was so insistent, and quite frankly your visiting me might have caused some gossip among my colleagues. You're rather well-known, but I expect you realise that.'

'To my sorrow,' said Antony, hiding his irritation well enough.

'We'll walk together to the bus stop then, that is unless you want me to call you a taxi.' Maitland shook his head. 'You don't want to see Joanna, do you?' Terence added rather sharply. 'There's really nothing she can tell you.'

196

'I imagine her views echo your own to some extent,' said Antony, evading the question, he hoped, neatly enough.

'Yes, they do. And even if she believed in Owen implicitly she wouldn't make a good witness, you know. Too easily rattled.'

Antony made no reply to that and they went on their way in silence. The bus that would take him back to the city came along first, he said goodbye to his companion in rather an absent-minded way and boarded it.

Sir Nicholas would probably be already at Astroff's if he hadn't another engagement, and Antony was sorely tempted to join him there. But he knew well enough the kind of cross-examination he would have to undergo, and he wasn't ready for questions yet. Besides, he thought, if he didn't linger over the meal he's have time to fit in Primrose Ross before going back to the Stowes' flat at four o'clock to see Joanna. Primrose might not be in, but he was beginning to think that wouldn't matter. The only trouble was you could be as certain as you liked in your own mind but there was still the little matter of legal proof. He smiled rather sourly at that way of putting it. Proof was the only thing that mattered, and that was just what he hadn't got.

So he ate in a restaurant that he considered inferior, but it happened to be near the bus stop. It didn't really matter what the food was like that day, he was thinking far too hard to notice what he was eating. As soon as he had finished he called for the bill and retraced his steps to Bayswater. And again he was lucky, the door of Primrose Ross's flat was flung open almost as soon as he had knocked.

'Mr Maitland!' She recoiled a little at the sight of him. 'What on earth are you doing here?'

'Were you expecting someone else?' he asked.

'No, it's just that I'm so surprised to see it's you.'

'May I come in?'

'Yes, of course. Of course you may.' She backed away from the door as she spoke. 'It's not that I want to be inhospitable, Mr Maitland, but I know you think the libel action was all my fault. And now poor dear Elizabeth, I don't understand that at all.'

'The libel action died when Mrs Coke was murdered,' he explained gently. 'I'm engaged in quite a different matter now, Owen Barrie's defence.'

'Oh, then I should be glad to help you. I don't think that dreadful man should be allowed to get away with it.'

That seemed rather a contradictory statement. 'What dreadful man?' he asked.

'Why, Edward of course. Who else could it have been?'

'What do you think his motive was, Miss Ross?'

'Revenge, of course. It was their evidence that exposed him, and we know he wasn't – wasn't normal. I'm afraid what he did followed quite inevitably.'

'Did you attend the court on Thursday, Miss Ross, Thursday a week ago I mean? I know you were excused after you'd given your evidence.'

'No, I didn't come back. I knew quite well what those two were going to say, because Elizabeth had told me in the letter. I couldn't bear to hear all that repeated.'

'Yes, that's very natural I'm sure, but there was a brief report in the papers the next morning. I'm referring to the question of mine that concluded David Barrie's evidence.'

She frowned over that, obviously trying to remember. 'Something about Elizabeth having promised to marry Owen Barrie,' she said at last. 'And David told you it wasn't true. Well it couldn't have been, could it? She was still married to Edward. But I dare say he wanted to marry that girl in his office, Elizabeth told me all about her, so that was an added motive.'

'I said I was defending Owen Barrie, Miss Ross, not that I was trying to prove my former client guilty. In fact, if it had

198

come to that I should still have regarded him as my client, and it was only on receiving his assurance that he wouldn't need my services that I consented to act for Mr Barrie.'

'That sounds like some legalistic nonsense,' she said, and for once he was inclined to agree with her. 'Who else could it have been?' she demanded again.

'That's what I'm trying to find out.'

'Well, I can't help you.'

'Tell me again what you thought of Elizabeth Coke.'

'I don't see the point of that. She was a perfect lady, a very kind, gentle person.'

'Not at all sensual?' He chose the word Terence Stowe had used deliberately, thinking she would find it perhaps the least offensive.

'Where on earth did you get an idea like that? I'm sure Elizabeth was above all that sort of thing. Her nature was more – more spiritual,' said Primrose.

'And yet she married Edward Coke.'

'I'm sure she thought he was her kind of person, someone who would respect her.'

'I see. You know Owen Barrie don't you, and knew David?'

'Certainly.'

'And you didn't think that any special relationship had developed between Mr Owen Barrie and Mrs Coke?'

'If you mean what I think you mean, Mr Maitland, the answer is No. But if you mean, was there perhaps a special friendship between them, that's quite true. Owen is a respectable man, Elizabeth would feel safe with him. And of course we know all about David, he wasn't altogether a nice young man, but what happened was Edward's fault.' She paused a moment and then went on more insistently than he had expected, 'I still don't see what brought you here, Mr Maitland.'

'A desire for information,' he said rather wearily. And

their talk had been illuminating in its way, he thought, though it had brought him no nearer the proof he so badly needed. 'I'm only sorry to have wasted your time, Miss Ross,' he added. 'I should have expressed my sympathy before about the death of your friend.'

Her mood seemed to soften at the word. 'Yes, I shall miss her,' she admitted. 'It isn't every day one finds someone so congenial. And I wish you'd listen to me, Mr Maitland, about what really happened. To someone who knew them both, Edward and Elizabeth – it's all so obvious.'

It was also obvious, he thought, finding his way to the street again, that whatever was to happen in the future nothing would ever convince her that Elizabeth Coke had been anything but the perfect lady she described.

He had still some time to wait before the four o'clock deadline Desmond had set for his meeting with Joanna Stowe. He walked round there slowly, and succeeded in finding a cup of tea on the way over which he sat until the waitress grew impatient with him. That made him think of Chief Inspector Sykes and his words of warning; in disregarding them he found himself a minority of one, and the Chief Inspector was no fool, and neither was Sir Nicholas. Perhaps they were in the right of it after all. The thought did nothing to cheer him, because he didn't see any way now of clearing the matter up before the trial, and when that came on he must do his best for his client regardless of any consequences to himself. However, the thought wasn't helpful. He paid the bill and left a rather larger tip than the amount warranted, and went on his way.

But when he reached his destination no-one came to the door despite repeated knocking. He waited around for more than a quarter of an hour, and once he thought he heard a movement inside and knocked again. But it was all to no avail, no-one answered.

When he got back to Kempenfeldt Square it was to find the study door open invitingly, so that Gibbs's disapproving remark that Sir Nicholas was expecting him (and you've kept him waiting rather a long time, said the butler's tone) was really unnecessary.

He wasn't surprised to find Jenny there with his uncle and aunt and all of them looking rather expectant, but he was tired and his shoulder was hurting him, and his greeting lacked something of the usual careful politeness that he used at least towards Vera. 'Where the carcase is, there shall the eagles be gathered together,' he said.

Jenny said, 'Oh, Antony!' reproachfully. Vera smiled her grim smile. Sir Nicholas, very much at his ease in his favourite chair, remarked only:

'You left chambers quite early this morning after receiving a telephone call from Mr Barleycorn.' He didn't share his nephew's gift for mimicry, but Antony was in no doubt that his uncle was quoting Mr Mallory. 'Naturally we formed our own opinion as to what you were doing, and you find us all agog to hear the result of your activities.'

'Damn all,' said Antony briefly. And then, relenting, 'Actually I'm very glad to find you all here together, because I badly want a counsel of war.'

Sir Nicholas cocked a knowledgeable eye at him. 'It's a little early,' he remarked, 'but I think you could do with a drink.'

Vera was on her feet before he could get up. 'Do the honours,' she said.

'Thank you, my dear. Am I to take it, Antony, that this idea you spoke of, this idea that was too vague to explain, has borne some fruit?'

'You're mixing your metaphors again Uncle Nick,' said

Antony. 'And it all depends on what you mean by fruit.'

'Don't equivocate, my boy.'

Antony sank onto the sofa beside Jenny, and didn't reply until his glass of sherry was in his hand. Then he said, 'I mean, I think I know who killed Elizabeth Coke and David Barrie, but I haven't a chance in the world of proving it.'

'Not Owen Barrie?' demanded Sir Nicholas.

'No, and not Edward Coke either, in spite of Primrose Ross's very vehemently expressed opinion to that effect.'

'Who then?'

'Terence Stowe.'

'The surgeon? You're going to have to explain that, Antony.'

'That's what I want to do, but don't go thinking I've got any proof to lay neatly before you, because I haven't. It's a matter of opinion. I prefer to call it pure deduction, but you may not agree with that.'

'Tell your story,' said his uncle, 'and let's see.'

'Very well.' He drank a little more sherry, put the glass down beside him and possessed himself firmly of Jenny's hand. 'You don't know, Vera, and neither do you, Jenny, that Chief Inspector Sykes came to see me the other day.' He saw Vera glance sharply at Sir Nicholas and added hurriedly, 'We couldn't discuss the case of course, not strategy anyway, but one thing he said – and I hope I'm not going back on my promise in telling you – was that perhaps I'd started the whole thing by the question I asked David Barrie in court that Thursday afternoon.'

'Lot of nonsense,' said Vera gruffly.

'Not altogether. You could take that two ways, as meaning that either Owen Barrie or Edward Coke was so jealous that the murders followed as a matter of course. But the jealousy, if it existed, might not have been confined to those two.'

'An interesting speculation,' said Sir Nicholas cordially.

'Well, I wondered you see, whether perhaps Edward Coke had been wrong in considering his wife a frigid woman. I'm pretty sure now, after what I've learned today, that she was just the opposite. I've had various descriptions of her, sensual, making a play for every man she saw, man-eater, and so on.'

'You'll forgive me for interrupting,' said Sir Nicholas, 'but you must have had some basis for this conclusion of yours.'

'Only that I thought that no completely unemotional woman could have inspired as much devotion as she seemed to have done. Or – and here you'll have to forgive me, Uncle Nick – could have deceived even her hard-bitten man of law.'

'*Touché,*' murmured his uncle.

'Well, that's so much water under the bridge, but may I remind you that, though my own observations and everything I've heard of Owen Barrie inclined me to believe that he's an old-fashioned man with old-fashioned moral values, he isn't exactly an innocent, and she took him in too. She played the role of a very gentle, feminine woman where she thought it might be effective.'

'As she did with me.' Sir Nicholas agreed cordially.

'I'm not trying to rub it in,' Antony protested, 'but in this one instance I was right and you were wrong. What I'm getting at is, I did wonder whether it reflected her real feelings.'

'We're accepting Edward Coke's word, however, that she refused to share his bed after the first few months of their marriage.'

'Yes, I don't think he attracted her at all. I think her motive for marrying him was purely mercenary, and when she knew Aunt Harriet hadn't made him her heir she cast about for the best way of getting rid of him. If there hadn't been the possibility of hooking Owen Barrie she probably would have been tempted to wait, but he was rich, too good a catch for her to risk his changing his mind. So she started looking very thoroughly into the question of divorce. She may even have consulted a lawyer – not Bellerby – but that's something we may never know. Anyway, she came up with this idea about exceptional depravity, and David Barrie agreed to help her prove it. We know what his reward was to be, or rather what she led him to believe. But Terence Stowe, when I first talked to him, displayed an uncommon knowledge of the laws concerning divorce for someone outside the profession who had never had to take advantage of them ... in any case, may I remind you, they have been changed very recently'.

'Even I knew that,' murmured his uncle. Antony flashed him a smile, but he was engrossed in his story now.

'That was the first point that put me on my guard about him,' he said. 'That was before the murders, and I didn't suspect him of anything further than of having perhaps had an affair with her. But when I talked to Sykes he let slip another bit of information, that though Elizabeth Coke had been stabbed a number of times, it was the first blow that killed her. That, as I know very well, is not at all easy to accomplish.'

'We must bow to your superior knowledge, of course,' said Sir Nicholas dryly.

'In this instance, sir, I think you may. It meant, you see, that she must have died practically instantaneously, or the doctors would have found their task more difficult.'

'And was David Barrie, too, killed in this masterly fashion?'

'No.'

'I don't understand how they could tell,' Jenny complained.

'Elizabeth was stabbed and died almost immediately, so that there was little or no bleeding from the other wounds.

In David's case there was nothing to show which of several of his wounds had proved fatal. There'd been some bleeding –'

'Yes, I think we all understand you,' said Sir Nicholas, who had been watching Jenny's face.

'I was only trying ... well, as I say, that was the point I'd reached by this morning, but I've been to see both Terence Stowe and the Walpoles ... and Primrose Ross too, and there was one small point to my talk with her, but I'll come to that later. I found the Walpoles, whom I saw separately, more willing to discuss Elizabeth's character now.'

'Afraid of a libel action?' asked Vera.

'I don't think that was it altogether. Anyway, what I learned from Roland was what I've already told you, that Elizabeth was no saint. Fran Walpole confirmed that, but she also said to me that she was my best source of information because she had no cause to be jealous. She didn't want to answer questions about who else might have been involved with Elizabeth, but the Stowes and the Walpoles seemed to have been the Cokes' closest friends, so I couldn't help taking her remark to mean that perhaps Joanna Stowe had some cause to feel resentful towards the dead woman.'

'Might have been mistaken about that,' Vera pointed out.

'Yes, I know, but you see it confirmed what I was already thinking.'

'It is always dangerous, Antony, to have a preconceived idea,' said Sir Nicholas.

'Seems to have had some basis though,' said Vera, promptly changing sides. 'This business of Mr Stowe knowing all about the divorce laws, Antony. I take it you're implying he'd discussed it with Elizabeth?'

'Yes, that's just what I do think. I mean if he'd wanted a divorce himself by any chance there'd be no need to go to those lengths. It's all quite simple once you get past the three-year mark.'

'What happened when you talked to Stowe himself?' asked Sir Nicholas.

'He admitted he'd had a fling with Elizabeth some time ago. I think those were his very words, and I think I can quote verbatim the rest of what he said. That it was over long since, and no hard feelings on either side.'

'Why did he tell you as much as that I wonder?'

'He isn't a man who is always very careful what he says, and he backs himself into a corner sometimes without realising it. That happened in another way too.'

'How was that?'

'Both Roland Walpole and Terence Stowe took the same view, ostensibly, of the case against Owen Barrie. That he was obviously guilty but might get away with a lesser charge – about which they were both understandably vague – in view of the extreme provocation.'

'But –' started Sir Nicholas.

'Yes, I know, Uncle Nick, that's what I'm coming to. I asked Walpole how he knew about Barrie's motive, and he said Owen had phoned him that evening about nine o'clock, to tell him about his talk with David. I must admit that Owen Barrie never mentioned it to me, but it's a matter that I can easily check and I don't think Roland was lying about it.'

'Seems unlikely in the circumstances,' said Vera.

'That's what I think. And this is what I mean about Terence backing himself into a corner, he made the same comment about Owen Barrie's motive, and he said he'd come back to court that Thursday, even though in view of his professional duties he'd been excused further attendance, and heard my question and David's reaction to it. That was reported in the newspaper account the next morning without comment, and Primrose Ross had seen that, but she couldn't make head or tail of it.'

'I think from your description, my dear boy, that probably Terence Stowe is rather more intelligent than this Miss Ross.'

'Oh, undoubtedly, all the same, Uncle Nick, think about it. The most that could be deduced from question and answer, and Elizabeth's denials, was that the two of them had lied about their future intentions. Elizabeth, in fact, made a very affecting story of it. No one could have deduced as much as Terence seemed to have done from all that, but if he had some special interest in Elizabeth it might have made him suspicious.'

'I think I see what you're getting at now. You think Stowe knew all the time about the arrangement with David, but didn't care about that.'

'Somebody said Elizabeth regarded David as negligible. That might well have been Terence Stowe's attitude as well.'

'So you're saying that if she were involved with Owen Barrie he'd regard it more seriously.'

'Yes, that's it exactly.'

'But this Terence Stowe, as I understand it, is a married man.'

'Yes, but I think he intended the affair to continue. I think she told him she wanted her freedom, but he was the only one she really cared about.'

'You're guessing, Antony.'

'Yes, I know, and I'm sorry because I realise it annoys you. But at this point I have to.'

'Well, for the moment we'll excuse you,' said Sir Nicholas magnanimously. Vera grinned in her nephew's direction.

'Means he's curious,' she explained, which Antony and Jenny, of course, already knew quite well.

'All right then. Terence thought the affair with David

207

would be terminated when the divorce was granted, but a possible marriage with Owen Barrie would be a different matter, it would effectively put a stop to Stowe's liaison with Elizabeth. So I think he put himself in her place, and realised that if it were true she'd want to set herself right in Owen's eyes that evening, and he went and watched the house. He saw her arrive and he saw her leave and then he confronted her. Perhaps they had some conversation, perhaps she tried to convince him that there was nothing in his fears, but I don't think she was successful. He stabbed her and pushed the body into the shadow so that she wouldn't be found immediately.'

'But why then Kill David as well?' asked Jenny. She'd been listening with her usual attention, but it wasn't often she interrupted one of these sessions.

'Elizabeth had been deceiving him. She might want love but she wanted money more. I think Terence Stowe could visualise David as part of that deception, could imagine their laughing together about his simple-mindedness. It may have been pure chance that he encountered David in Avery Mews, or he may have gone there deliberately because he'd heard him speak of it as a short cut. My conjecturing doesn't go as far as that, Uncle Nick, for which you may be grateful.'

'I am', said his uncle. 'But if you're right about all this, why should so skilled a murderer as Terence Stowe have taken more than one blow to despatch his second victim?'

'Elizabeth was facing him. David had turned away, and the only reason I can think of for that is that he saw what was coming and was trying to escape. A moving target . . . the thing is, what do you think of the case I've made out?'

'Would you call it a case? If it be against reason, let me remind you, it is of no force in law.'

'Let's leave Coke out of this . . . the original Coke, I mean,' Antony pleaded. 'As to whether I'd call it a case, not in the

208

legal sense, I told you that in the beginning. I mean' – his eyes went from Sir Nicholas to Vera – 'what do you both think of my ideas?'

'In your eyes at least I'm sure they form a basis on which to work,' said Sir Nicholas, rather unkindly. 'The question is, what do you propose to do about it?'

'That's why I want to talk to you, Uncle Nick.' There was a tinge of desperation in Antony's voice. 'What can I do?'

'Find the knife,' his uncle suggested. 'I take it that these conjectures of yours include one to the effect that Mr Terence Stowe extracted the one that was used deliberately from the Barries' kitchen.'

'I'm sorry I forgot that bit. Yes, of course that's what I think, too much of a coincidence otherwise. Besides, it would fit in with David's murder ... don't you think? If Terence's suspicions were right, Elizabeth would be punished, and David would be punished for conspiring with her as he saw it, and this was a way of punishing Owen too for being the man she wanted to marry.'

'Yes, that has a certain weird logic,' said his uncle thoughtfully. 'My advice to you remains the same, find the knife.'

'I don't suppose for a minute that's possible. He'll have disposed of it long since.'

'I hope you're not going to try –' But at that moment he was interrupted by a tap on the door, followed immediately by Gibbs's entrance.

'There's a young lady here to see Mr Maitland,' he said, more reproachfully than ever. 'I told her that at the moment he was occupied, but she was very insistent. I might almost say, Sir Nicholas, that there is something distraught about her.'

Knowing Gibbs, the description "young lady" might cover anything from a child of six years old to a woman of at least fifty. All the same Maitland, thinking of the door that he had found closed against him that afternoon, was visited by a sudden premonition. 'Did she give her name, Gibbs?' he asked, so forcefully that the old man's attitude became even stiffer.

'I should not otherwise have troubled you, Mr Maitland. She is a Mrs Joanna Stowe. Mrs Terence Stowe I gathered when I questioned her.'

Antony was on his feet. 'If you wish to see this lady, my boy,' said Sir Nicholas, 'may I suggest that you do so here. Vera and I will go upstairs with Jenny.'

'No, don't do that. Don't you see, Uncle Nick, if I'm right, if I'm anywhere near right – I need witnesses to what she's going to say.'

'All of us?' asked Sir Nicholas, looking round the room as though he half expected to see a horde of friends and relations hiding in the corners. 'I think I should remind you, Antony, that if you are right –'

'I know, no place for ladies. But Vera was too many years at the bar not to have heard everything by now, and Jenny put up a pretty good case the other day for not being kept in the dark. Still, if you'd like to go upstairs, love –'

'Not on your life,' said Jenny, and gave him one of the special smiles that were usually reserved for their times alone together. 'Do you think I could possibly sit there all by myself, wondering? Of course I'll stay.'

'All right then. Unless, of course, it seems that she'd talk better with fewer people present.'

'In that case,' said Vera, 'Jenny and I will retreat. Don't worry.'

'All right then,' said Antony again. 'Will you show Mrs Stowe in, Gibbs?'

Gibbs, who had been drinking all this in with who knows what disparaging thoughts in his mind, turned without a word and went out into the hall. A moment later he was back, 'Mrs Stowe, Sir Nicholas,' he announced, and retreated shutting the door firmly behind him.

But he had been quite right, there was a certain wildness about Joanna's appearance that hadn't been there when Antony saw her previously. She was still wearing a rather crumpled pink frock, and her hair was still limp and lifeless, but she was breathing rather deeply and quite clearly in the grip of some very violent emotion. 'Mr Maitland!' she said, coming towards him as though there was no-one else in the room.

'Good afternoon, Mrs Stowe.' He would have liked to come straight to the point with her, to get out of her whatever story it was she had come to tell, but there were some things he could bring himself to do and others that were quite impossible. In this case . . . 'This is my wife, Jenny, Mrs Stowe. My aunt, Lady Harding, and my uncle, Sir Nicholas Harding.'

Just for a moment that brought her up short. She ignored the two women but looked at Sir Nicholas closely. 'You took Elizabeth's part,' she said accusingly.

'Yes, Mrs Stowe, we've met before in court,' Sir Nicholas agreed.

'Well, it doesn't matter now, nothing matters now!'

'I think it would be as well if you sat down, Mrs Stowe,' said Sir Nicholas, who obviously thought it was time to interject a note of sanity into the proceedings. 'You'll be quite comfortable on the sofa there, beside Mrs Maitland. And if you would like to see my nephew alone –'

'It doesn't matter,' she repeated. But she seated herself obediently and Sir Nicholas was able to sit down himself, leaving Antony on his feet with his back to the empty hearth.

'I tried to see you this afternoon, Mrs Stowe,' Maitland told her.

'Yes, I know. At least, I knew you were coming and I heard someone at the door. But I wasn't ready to talk to you then. I'm afraid I'd been crying. I knew all along, you see, that Terence had been unfaithful to me, but I never thought I'd hear him say it. And once other people know, that makes a difference. You can understand that, can't you?'

'You say your husband admitted to you –?'

'No, I don't mean that at all. I was in the flat when you were talking to him, Mr Maitland – he went straight out with you otherwise I dare say he'd have found me after you left – and I tiptoed out into the hall and the door was a little ajar.'

'I see. So you couldn't help overhearing –'

'I listened quite deliberately,' she said firmly. 'I think I had a right to know. Not that I didn't know almost everything already,' she added sadly.

'I'm not quite sure what you're going to tell me, Mrs Stowe, but I do think I ought to point out to you that we aren't alone, there's no question of my keeping anything you say to me in confidence. A wife can't be compelled to give evidence against her husband, but even if you change your mind, with four people present –'

'Then you do know already,' she said.

'Not as much as I'd like to,' Antony told her.

'Well, that's what I'm here for ... to tell you. Terence went back to court that afternoon, the Thursday afternoon the day Elizabeth died. We didn't have to go but he said he was interested. And then when we came home he was in a dreadful state, but he wouldn't tell me then what was the matter. Only he went out as soon as we'd had dinner, and I didn't see him again until turned eleven o'clock. I was terribly worried by that time, as you can imagine, and when he came in ... there was blood on his shirt!'

'What happened then, Mrs Stowe?'

'I asked him what had happened, and now I wish I hadn't because he told me ... everything,' she said. 'That when you'd asked David in court whether he knew his father was going to marry Elizabeth when she was free he became suspicious of her motives. He was quite open with me, well, he knew I guessed anyway I suppose. He said she'd been his mistress for quite a long time, and she promised that things would go on as they always had. But if she really meant to marry Owen . . . you can see he felt he had to find out.'

'So he took steps to do so?'

'Yes, he went out and watched the house, Owen's house. He thought if Elizabeth went there that evening it would be sufficient confirmation of his fears. And she did go, and he waylaid her when she left, and she tried to persuade him that everything was just the same as it had always been between them, but she couldn't explain the visit to Owen, you see. So at last, when she saw she was getting nowhere with him, she told him everything, how she'd plotted with David but was going to – to ditch him, she said, when the divorce case was over, and she had been going to marry Owen because he had money, only now it seemed he'd have nothing more to do with her. So things could go on with Terence just as they always had. I think that hurt him more than anything else.'

'Could you explain that, Mrs Stowe?'

'Just that he asked her straight out, "And supposing you had married Owen?" And she said quite openly, "I'm afraid it would all have been over between us, Terence, I couldn't have risked his finding out." And that's when he killed her.'

Antony took a moment to look around him. Jenny was sitting quite upright with her hands clasped in her lap, and she was a little paler than usual but otherwise calm. Vera, as befitted a member of the bar of many years standing, was listening with rapt interest, and no emotion at all. Sir Nicholas answered his nephew's glance with a look that might have been interpreted, thought Antony bitterly, in a hundred different ways. As annoyance that an unpleasant scene was being played out before Jenny and Vera, or even as congratulation that some of his guesses had been pretty near the mark. 'Did your husband tell you all this at that time, Mrs Stowe?' he asked his visitor gently.

'Oh yes of course, I told you he was quite open with me. And about David. That was pure accident, Avery Mews was his nearest way to the bus stop, and he hadn't taken the car that night. And when he saw David it just came over him that he'd been made a fool of, and as he said to me, "It's much easier the second time."'

If it occurred to Antony that there was an added motive, that David would have been a witness to Terence Stowe's presence in that part of the world, this was no time, he thought, to interrupt the flow of her narrative.

'In each case he took the weapon away with him. Did he bring it home?'

'Yes, he did, because he said if he threw it away any-where near the scene of the murders the police would be sure to find it and though he'd held it in his scarf he hadn't thought to put gloves on, and there might be fingerprints.'

'Just a moment, it was a warm night.'

'I didn't tell you, did I? He'd told me when he went out that he was going to a dinner, one of the medical societies, and he was in full evening dress. It was a silk scarf, he wrapped the knife in it afterwards so he could slip it in his pocket without the pocket being cut. And later that night he spent hours washing it.'

'Is the knife still at your flat?'

'No, I think he took it to the hospital with him. He said if he threw it into the river somebody would be sure to see, but he could slip it among the other knives in the little kitchen the nurses use sometimes and nobody would ever notice.'

'It seems nobody did,' Sir Nicholas commented. 'May I

214

put a question to you, madam? Was it a knife taken from Barrie's house?'

'Oh yes, indeed it was.'

'With the deliberate intention of implicating Owen Barrie?'

'No, that wasn't his idea then. He said he'd meant to strangle Elizabeth with his bare hands if he found she was guilty, as he called it. Only then he thought a knife might be even quicker and quieter, and he remembered that one night when he'd gone home with Owen they'd been locked out. Owen had left his key in his other suit, something like that, and so he let them in by the back door and Terence saw where the key was kept. Afterwards, of course, he was rather pleased about it, because after Owen was arrested it meant that the police wouldn't be looking for anybody else.'

'Got it very nearly right,' said Vera. Antony nodded in a depressed way, he wasn't enjoying his triumph. And suddenly Jenny surprised them all by saying in her quiet way:

'Mrs Stowe, you say your husband told you everything, but you've kept quiet about it ever since.'

Joanna Stowe turned and looked at her, a long look that Jenny said afterwards seemed to go through and through her. 'I think you might understand that,' she said at last. 'He's my husband, I couldn't give him away.'

'But now –'

'It's different now.'

'Because you know he was in love with Elizabeth Coke?'

'Not just that. I've known about that for a long time, and I suppose I'd come to terms with it. But it was different when nobody else knew, I couldn't stand other people knowing, you must see that. So when he talked to your husband this afternoon so openly I made up my mind.' She paused and in her turn looked all round the assembled

215

company. 'I understand the position,' she said, 'and I'm quite aware that I could refuse to testify if I wanted. And now I think I should like to make a statement to the police.'

Epilogue

'The only question that remains,' said Sir Nicholas at teatime on Sunday, though he made quite sure that the plate of buttered toast was empty before he spoke, 'is why she came to you, Antony, instead of going directly to Sykes.' As usual they were all having tea together in the Maitlands' living-room, and Antony, who had hoped for the weekend at least to forget the whole matter, wasn't at all pleased with the question.

It was Jenny who replied. 'I think that's quite obvious, Uncle Nick,' she said. 'Antony made a great impression on her when he questioned her about the libel action, that's why she came to him.'

'You may be right, my dear. Perhaps the lady is easily impressed,' said Sir Nicholas. 'But I think myself –'

'Any event, the result was the same,' said Vera, interrupting her husband in the interests of peace. She had seen Antony before in the throes of the depression that always seemed to follow the successful conclusion of a case, and though to her this seemed an illogical reaction she knew it was very real to him. 'Owen Barrie will be released tomorrow, Terence Stowe is helping the police with their enquiries, and Antony tells us that Chief Inspector Sykes telephoned him to say the knife had been found exactly where Mrs Stowe said it was. That seems to me to be very satisfactory.'

'You might add,' said Sir Nicholas idly, 'that Edward Coke's character is in a fair way to being vindicated. That seems to me one of the more satisfactory aspects of the matter.' If Vera wanted to spare his nephew's feelings he had no intention of disobliging her.

'Suppose now he'll marry that girl, what's her name, Mary Jerrold?' said Vera.

'Antony didn't tell you that bit,' said Jenny. 'It appears that Desmond Barleycorn is in love with her too. He thinks he may have a chance now that – how was it he put it, Antony? – now that Edward Coke isn't any longer completely unattainable.'

'Didn't know that,' said Vera. 'Good psychology though.'

'My dear, if we are to talk of psychology,' said Sir Nicholas, for once in his life with no great attention to logic, 'I think we must all rejoice that in this case at least Superintendent Briggs can have nothing to say to Antony's detriment.'

'Of course he can't, Uncle Nick,' said Jenny bristling.

'I think he might have tried,' said Sir Nicholas, unmoved by the contradiction. 'But all is well. With Vera and myself present I don't think even the Superintendent would think of suggesting that Antony had – what is the phrase you used, Vera? – rigged the evidence.'

Jenny was about to say indignantly, 'I was there too,' when she caught her husband's eye. Antony was laughing helplessly.

'It's just as you said, Uncle Nick,' he remarked, 'Vera *is* corrupting you.' And watched with no lessening of amusement as his uncle turned towards his wife to refute the charge, more indignantly than convincingly.